Bennett

Bennett

BOURBON & BLOOD
Book One

CHASITY BOWLIN

Bennett

Prologue

"What the hell is the meaning of this, Erica?" Mia demanded as she slapped the memo onto the desk.

The other woman pursed her perfectly lined and lacquered lips. "Where did you get that?"

"I am the one asking the questions here. Who do you think you are to come into my family's business and try to alter the very fabric of the company we've built?" She was more livid than she could recall being in a very long time.

The memo was fairly straightforward. It was a request to review a proposal to increase production by diluting the older barrels held in reserve with newer batches of bourbon. It would greatly increase the volume of their product, but it would decimate the quality.

"Samuel asked for people to think outside the box," Erica replied coolly. "Profits were down last year, Mia. Your marketing plan didn't work."

Mia clenched her fists and tried to rein in her temper. She had a lot of issues with the other woman, and not all of them were professional. "Profits were down because another distillery, that is our direct competition, was plastered all over the news on a daily basis for months. Just because some asshat production line workers managed to pull off the crime of the century and steal more than a hundred thousand dollars' worth of bourbon and that's all every news outlet in the state can talk about! That is the kind of publicity and advertising that cannot be purchased."

"Regardless, we need to be looking ahead and not behind. You're too mired in tradition, Mia. You're losing sight of what this company could be," Erica said with a smug smile. "Your father will listen to me. We both know that."

Mia smiled in return, though the expression was loaded with venom. "*We* all know, and by *we*, I mean everyone, that more of your work is accomplished under my father's desk than at your own. Just because you've managed to get him into your bed, don't make the mistake of thinking you can control him. Samuel Darcy will never compromise Fire Creek Distilleries."

"You don't run the show, Mia. Neither do your brothers!" Erica snapped hotly.

"My brothers and I, together, have controlling interest in this company. As long as we stick together, there's not a damn thing you can do about it. And I might not be a daddy's girl, but don't think for a single second that I can't get rid of you."

"Are you threatening me?" Erica fired back. "My attorney will be very happy to hear that."

"I don't threaten. I'm offering you a piece of professional advice, and as it's coming from someone who owns a portion of this company, you should take it. Learn your place, stay within the bounds you've been given, and you can work here to your heart's content—or until my father's eye wanders again. That won't take long, by the way. But overstep again, and your career here will be over. Are we understood?"

Erica glared at her. "This isn't over."

"Oh, I think it is," Mia replied softly. "You are here to take customers and guests on tours, to talk up the bourbon industry like it's a bit of royalty while you wear the charitably given title of Assistant VP of Marketing. You are not now, nor will you ever be, part of this distillery. Remember that." Mia took the mic drop moment and waltzed out. She left the door open in her wake, but it was only seconds later that she heard it slam with considerable force. It was followed by the sound of breaking glass. A full-on tantrum was in process and she felt strangely good about being at the heart of it.

One

Mia marched down the hallway, her heels clicking on the hardwood floor. There was no denying that she was angry. It showed in the length and force of her stride, the rigid posture of her spine and in the fire burning in her whiskey-brown eyes. Anger didn't even begin to cover what she was feeling.

Grasping the door handle, she opened the door to her brother's office and strode in. Clayton was behind his desk, tie loosened, hair wild, and a pair of glasses perched on the end of his nose. "Those are new," she remarked.

Clayton looked up, sighed, removed the glasses and set them aside. "Getting old is hell," he muttered as he glanced at the blinking light on his phone. "Do I want to answer that?"

"Is it Erica?"

Clayton sighed again, this time with much more feeling. "I don't like her. Quentin doesn't like her. No one who works here likes her. But I can't fire her for being a bitch. Even if I could, I can't fire her because she is sleeping with our father."

Mia shuddered with distaste. "What about trying to undermine the quality of Fire Creek Bourbon?"

Clayton eased back in his chair. "We might have something with that. Do you have proof?"

Mia laid the memo on his desk. "She's trying to talk Dad into increasing the volume produced by mixing barrels we've been aging for more than thirty years with the newer stuff."

"Fucking idiot."

"Yes. Both of them. I know the waiting list is creating pressure, and I know that right now we've been unable to meet the demand for our bourbon, but in terms of our worth, that's not a bad thing," Mia said and plopped down in the chair that faced his desk.

She loved the distillery. She'd loved it even as a little kid. Rough-hewn beams and aged brick allowed the age and the history of the building to shine through. It wasn't state of the art, but in the back, where the magic happened, it was an odd but working mix of new and old. So much of bourbon production was tradition, but there was definitely a bit of science involved. Everyone thought it was just whiskey, a simple mixture of corn and rye, cooked and fermented. But the complexities of flavor, the chemical processes that took place in the charred oak barrels as the liquid swelled and receded in each vessel for no less than four years, with Kentucky's naturally fluctuating weather, that was where the real magic happened. That was where it stopped being just alcohol, just a method to achieve inebriation, and instead became something that defined a lifestyle and a culture. Erica, if she didn't take her head out of her ass, would never understand that. Bourbon was more than a name and more than a price tag.

"I can't get rid of her for this," Clayton replied. "It's

stupid. I can squash this little proposal like a bug, but I can't fire her for having a bad idea that was never implemented."

Mia rolled her eyes. "Can we fire her for aspiring to be a real housewife?"

"I wish. I know she gets under your skin," he said reasonably. "It bugs me too when he flaunts his mistresses, but to put her right here in the middle of the family business is a lot. I'll talk to him. Maybe what we need to do with Erica is find her a better job elsewhere. She'd be hell on wheels as a sales rep. She'd be good at that."

"She's quite experienced at selling things," Mia added cattily. "Fine. Talk to him. Or find some way to send her packing. She's not going to use her feminine wiles to dismantle this company or to destroy the reputation we've built."

Clayton nodded. "I'll work on it, and you should go home. Knock off early. Go pick up a bottle of wine and relax. We've had more tours this week than we've had in ages."

"Breeder's Cup," she reminded him. "They always come in then. But I am going to take off. And wine sounds like a fantastic idea." It was the only thing about her Friday night that sounded good. Otherwise, it was going to be just a sad repeat of the one before it, and the one before that one. She'd spend some time reading to her mother. Most people called it a waste of time, and sometimes Mia agreed, but other times she liked to imagine that Patricia could still understand them. And after she finished reading a few chapters of the mysteries that Patricia had always preferred, she might indulge in a steamy romance novel for herself. More than likely, she'd just be so damned tired she'd go to bed.

"Are you happy, Mia?"

The question caught her off guard, especially coming from Clayton. For as long as she could remember, Clayton had been all logic and reason. Calm and even-keeled, she thought of him as her own personal Spock. "No. Are you?"

He laughed at that. "My wife left me. The distillery is bleeding money for repairs and maintenance, mostly because our idiot father mortgaged it to the hilt. He also refuses to listen to my ideas that are the product of the very expensive education he paid for...no, Mia. I'm not happy. But I at least had a shot at Annalee and I couldn't make it work, but at least we got to try."

She knew where the conversation was going and she couldn't. She just couldn't. "Don't, Clayton. Just don't. It's ancient history."

"Not that ancient. You two might not talk to each other, but you're still the talk of the town, Fontaine's very own star-crossed lovers."

"It doesn't matter. Even if I did want to dig up that particular skeleton," she said flatly. "He has moved on. I wouldn't mess that up for him even if it were an option."

Clayton tapped his pen on the desk. "Why wasn't it an option before? You both live right here. His house is less than two miles from ours on the same damned road, Mia. Why not?"

"Mama," she said simply.

"We can hire people to take care of Mama. She can have round-the-clock care. You don't have to carry that burden alone, Mia. What's the real reason?"

"My reasons—" She stopped, took a deep breath and let it out. "My reasons are mine to share as I choose. And right now, I'm choosing not to. I'll see you Monday...or Sunday if you decide to come for dinner and bring the munchkin."

"We'll be there," he replied. "All Darcys are creatures of habit."

They were creatures of misery, she thought. Not a one of them was happy. It's what came of being the fruit of a poisoned tree. Keeping that happy little gem of wisdom to herself, Mia walked around the desk, kissed her brother's cheek, and said, "I'm going home. It's a weekend. That's what people do. You ought to yourself."

"I'm picking the kiddo up at seven after her dance practice," he promised. "Then the only work I'll be doing is keeping up with her."

"I love you, Clay. You're an awesome big brother, even if you are a huge pain in the ass sometimes."

Mia laughed as she ducked the pen he'd chucked at her. She left on a much lighter note than she'd entered. But that was what Clayton did for everyone except himself. She wondered briefly who he unburdened himself to. Shelving that thought until she could do something about it, she gathered her keys and purse and headed for her car. It was getting ready to storm, and she wanted to get her wine and maybe some chocolate chip cookies before heading home.

The rain was coming down in an endless sheet as Bennett Hayes parked his truck in the small lot outside Fontaine, Kentucky's only grocery store. It was Friday, and he had the whole weekend to himself, free from Emmitt's bitching, Carter's whining and Savannah's endless list of chores. To celebrate his weekend of freedom and isolation, he needed beer.

Dashing through the automatic doors, he stopped

long enough to wipe the water from his face. When he opened his eyes, he regretted it instantly.

Less than two feet in front of him was the last woman in the world he wanted to run into. Somehow, in a town of only a couple thousand people, they managed to avoid one another successfully, most of the time. When they didn't, it was always awkward and charged with tension. Today was no exception. Even the electrical hum that always buzzed in the air of the grocery store went dead quiet. A pin could have dropped and it would have sounded like a bomb.

It wasn't just the silence. There were all of five other people in the small store. Every single one of them stopped what they were doing and watched the two of them with bated breath. He didn't really care. His eyes were drawn to her. He took in every detail, from the new lighter streaks in her hair, to the fact that she'd put on a little weight, but it only made her more appealing. As if he needed that.

Even though it had been ten years since they'd uttered more than a polite hello to one another, looking at her was still like a punch in the gut. He watched her face, saw the shock of recognition, and then the slight firming of her lips and tightening of her jaw. There might have been something else in between, a flash of regret, a slight hint of longing. But it wouldn't matter. It *couldn't* matter. That particular bed had been made a long time ago and they both had to lie in it alone.

After the longest moment, she inclined her head slightly. "Bennett."

He could tell it cost her to utter the word. Once upon a time, she'd uttered it with ease, in a dozen different ways —exasperatedly, tenderly, passionately. Now it sounded forced and cold. "Mia," he acknowledged. "How are you?"

She smiled but it didn't reach her eyes. There was a sadness in them instead, and loneliness. Or maybe that was just wishful thinking on his part.

"I'm just fine. You?" Her response was polite and so fucking impersonal he wanted to shake her.

"No complaints," he replied easily. Except that he missed her. Every goddamn day even after ten years, he missed her. "How's your mother?"

The question brought a flash of sadness to her eyes. It was a tough subject for her. It always had been. Patricia Darcy had always been a vibrant and beautiful woman, until their senior year in high school. While he and Mia had been sneaking around, fooling no one but themselves, her life had changed, turning on a fateful and bitter dime. One rainy day in late summer, she'd wrapped her car around a tree and the massive head trauma she'd endured had changed things for everyone.

If he were going to be honest with himself, he could look back and see then that things with Mia had changed. Her laugh had become less frequent, her smile a little more guarded. When she answered, her shuttered expression was familiar. "She's about the same—she has good days and bad days. Your family is well?"

"They're just fine," he said. "Savannah keeps us all hopping."

She smiled at that, but it didn't reach her eyes. "Some things never change," she said.

And other things turned on a dime, he thought bitterly, including the woman in front of him. "Consistency is always a good thing," he replied. It was an unintentional dig, but a direct hit nonetheless. He saw it in the slight flinch and the shuttering of her gaze.

"I should go," she said, lifting the grocery bags from her cart. "I need to get home before the creek gets any higher."

He said nothing, just moved aside so that she could pass without having to touch him. But he could smell the barest hint of her perfume. Looking over his shoulder, he watched her cross the parking lot and climb behind the wheel of her little sports car. The personalized plate on the front of it read *Darcy3*.

It was a glaring reminder of why they weren't together. She was a Darcy and he was a Hayes and never the twain shall meet.

Cursing under his breath, he turned and found himself under the scrutiny of Miss Helen. She'd been working behind the counter of that grocery store since he was a boy. Her glasses were thicker, the bifocals stronger, and you might have to talk a little louder to her to be understood, but she still didn't miss much.

"You two!" she said. "I swear! Never seen more hard-headed people in my life!"

Bennett didn't say anything, just walked back to the cooler and grabbed a six-pack of beer. After he paid for his purchase and tolerated a heaping dose of Miss Helen's disapproval, he went back out to his truck and climbed behind the wheel.

He sat there for a moment, replaying the vision of her in his mind. Dark hair, damp and curling around her face, her pink lips parted in surprise as her dark eyes widened, and that slight flush that had crept over her cheeks—it reminded him of other times that she'd blushed for him, over the outrageous things he'd said to her, over their painfully inept fumbling in the back seat of his father's old Buick.

She was as beautiful as she had been when he'd first fallen head over heels for her and just as off limits to him.

"Fuck me," he said bitterly, and turned the key in the ignition with more force than necessary. The truck's engine roared to life, but when he pulled out of the parking lot, he drove with care, with caution—just like he did everything else in life.

Two

Mia downshifted again, the car speeding over the wet road. The slowpoke in front of her in the black SUV had finally picked up the pace. She was going too fast in the rain, but she needed to get away, to outrun all the hurt and anger that boiled up inside her just from seeing him again.

It wasn't his fault. It wasn't even her fault. There was just too much bad blood between their families for anyone to ever let them be. Rather than destroy everyone's lives, they'd settled for destroying their own. *It hadn't been his choice.* The insidious little voice whispered in her mind, reminding her that she'd made the choice for them both.

Bennett hadn't fought for her because she'd never told him the truth. She'd kept all that locked up inside herself and had gone along with her father's plan. She'd been a coward then and she was still one today, she thought bitterly.

God, he looked good! It wasn't fair, she thought. Somehow the beautiful boy she'd known had turned into the sexiest man alive. He was chiseled and lean, and even through the damp T-shirt he'd worn, she could see every muscle. She'd also caught the tantalizing glimpse of a tattoo, some strange tribal design that might have had some deeper meaning or might have been the result of a drunken dare from Carter. She'd been told about the tattoo but had never seen it in person. With dark, curling hair that refused to be tamed by any product and deep green eyes, Bennett was more than just handsome.

The beard was new. He'd started sporting one recently and it worked, framing his mouth and highlighting the rugged bone structure beneath. She wondered briefly what Lacey thought of it, but then she reminded herself that it wasn't her business. Who he dated, who he married, shouldn't matter to her. She was the one who'd made the choice to let him go. Of course that didn't ease the ache inside her or dissipate the anger.

"Goddamn him," she muttered.

As she rounded the bend, her eyes widened in terror. In the middle of the road, parked to block both lanes, was the same black SUV that had left her in the dust a few minutes earlier. With its massive deer guard, it took up nearly the entire road.

It was instinct more than anything else that had Mia turning the wheel. The car spun out of control, doing at least a couple of three sixties on the wet asphalt as she fought the wheel. It was no use. The car kept going, coasting sideways toward the soft shoulder. If she hit the mud there the wheels would sink and the car would roll.

It shouldn't have been possible in that split second for those kinds of thoughts to enter her mind but they did. Swerving hard, she managed to bring the car to a stop, the rear wheels resting in the mud, the back end of the car hanging over the ledge where there was a gap in the guardrail.

Breathing hard, adrenaline pumping in her veins, she didn't have to look to know that she was in a bad place. A glance at the rearview mirror showed her there was nothing behind the car but a gray, leaden sky. If she tried to push forward and the wheels were stuck, it could send her sliding backward even further toward the precipice. Getting out was the only option.

Needing answers about just how dire her predicament was, Mia reached for the door handle to look out. With every movement and every gust of wind, the car rocked ominously. She was closer to the edge than she'd realized. Opening the door slightly, she peered behind her and saw that the back wheels were barely resting on solid ground. Even at the thought, the mud beneath the wheels slipped a bit. Not so solid, she thought worriedly.

The other vehicle started, the engine painfully loud. Mia closed her door and looked forward, anticipating some offer of assistance. Rather than a cautious approach and the helpful offer of a tow, the car closed in on her until the vehicles were bumper to bumper. Even with her foot on the brake, the car was pushed relentlessly backward.

Mia didn't scream. She was too stunned by what was happening. The dark tinted windows of the other vehicle were impenetrable. She couldn't even see that a person was inside it, much less what they looked like. In a last ditch effort, Mia grasped the handle of the parking brake and jerked it up. It didn't even slow them down.

The tires slipped in the mud, sending it showering up over the car. Then they slipped beyond the ledge completely. It teetered for a moment, nothing but air beneath the rear wheels. The little sports car that she loved rolled down the bank toward the rushing creek below.

The airbag exploded into her face with enough force

to knock the wind out of her. The sunglasses that she favored, even in the rain, broke on impact, the frame slicing into her skin just above her eyebrow.

The car flipped again, belly up this time. The windshield shattered into tiny little cubes and rained down on her, creating a dozen stinging cuts. Her right elbow slammed into the console, the pain of it exploding up her arm. Another roll, this one to the side and Mia's left hand, which had still been on the wheel, twisted free and connected forcefully with the steering column. The car slid nose down into the creek. The water rushed in, frigid cold and moving fast as it spilled into the car.

Mia tried to scream, but couldn't. The seat belt had locked so tight it was all she could do to breathe. The blood from her forehead was running down her face, spilling into her mouth. She spit it out and tried again. The sound that escaped her wasn't even human, just a keening animalistic cry prompted by pain and fear.

The car shifted again from the force of the water rushing around it and pouring into it. It sank fully into the swollen creek, swept by the current. Panicked, Mia reached beneath the icy surface and tugged at the seat belt. Her right hand wasn't working. Her fingers wouldn't move the way they were supposed to, and fumbling with the latch with her left hand was simply not working. Whether it was the water or her own numb, shaking hands, it wouldn't give.

She was going to die, and it wasn't an accident.

The water surged around her, but she didn't feel the cold. Determined, she tried once more to free the seat belt. The button clicked as she pressed it, but it wouldn't give. The seatbelt remained firmly locked in place.

The water had reached her chin and she was having to keep her head tilted back to breathe. A broken sob escaped her. The car slipped deeper into the flowing creek, the waterline creeping higher and higher. Mia took one last gulping breath before it flowed over her entirely.

She'd closed her eyes against the sting of the freezing water, but they flew open when a pair of strong hands settled on her shoulders. Even in the murky water, she could see Bennett's face. For a split second, she wondered if she were hallucinating, or if she might already have died.

He reached past her and tugged at the seat belt. When it wouldn't give, he dug into his pocket for a knife. The blade eased past her, sawing through the fabric.

Her lungs burned. Then Bennett was gone. *He wouldn't leave her there.* Even as she thought it, he reappeared, lunging into the car almost entirely. His hands cupped her face and his mouth pressed to hers. Her lips parted, the last of her breath escaping. But then his mouth was on hers, his breath stealing into her.

A few more passes of the knife and the seat belt gave. She floated up from the seat and Bennet guided her through the broken window. When they broke the surface, she took a deep breath in and then met the hardened gaze of the man who'd saved her life. She wanted to say something to him, anything, but the words wouldn't come. Blackness closed in, the periphery of her vision narrowing to pinpoints until there was nothing.

Free balling under the borrowed scrubs he had on, Bennett was acutely aware of just how hard the plastic chairs of the waiting room were. After fishing Mia out of the creek, he'd had to leave her on the bank while he climbed back up, slipping and sliding on the muddy hillside until he could get back to his truck and his forgotten phone. Now, with his filthy clothes in the plastic bag beside his feet, and an inch of mud covering every part of him, he wanted a shower in the worst possible way, but first, he had to know she was okay.

Staring down at the floor, he scrubbed his hands over his face and tried to think of anything but how she'd looked. A dozen tiny little cuts, her lips bloodied, and he'd known without a doubt that her wrist was broken.

The doctor had assured him that it was the shock and the pain of her obviously broken wrist more than anything else that had rendered her unconscious. Bennett wanted to believe that, but he was half afraid to let himself.

A commotion at the door brought his head up and Bennett bit back a curse as he saw the Darcy brothers come barreling in. As a general rule, they were all good at simply ignoring one another, but with tensions running high, it was bound to be trouble.

Even as the thought entered his mind, Quentin looked over at him and his mouth twisted in a sneer. "What the hell are you doing here, Hayes? Did you have something to do with this, you son of a bitch?"

An elderly woman in the waiting room gasped and looked mightily offended at the language. Bennett rose to his feet. "If by 'something to do with it' you mean I saved your sister's fool neck, then yeah."

Quentin started toward him, fists clenched and teeth bared. Clayton grabbed his brother's arm and held him back.

"We're grateful for what you did, but it's probably best if you go now," Clayton said. "Samuel is on his way here, and that's a mess none of us want."

Clayton had always been the voice of reason, the calm

one, the eye in the center of the Darcy tornado. Bennett's pride stung at being dismissed, at being reminded that he wasn't permitted to be part of Mia's world, that he didn't belong. But at the same time, he recognized that causing a giant scene and creating more stress in her life wouldn't be good for any of them. It sucked being an adult. As a hot-headed teenager he would have just rammed his fist in Quentin's face and told Clayton to kiss his ass. A part of him still wanted to.

But those days were over. Bennett shoved his hands through his still wet hair. "I want to know how she is."

Clayton nodded. "I'll send word to you when we know something."

Bennett picked up his bag and exited the hospital. He'd just climbed behind the wheel of his truck when a limo pulled up and Samuel Darcy emerged from the back seat. His white hair was combed back neatly, his tie was still crisp and perfect. It perfectly encapsulated their lives. That son of a bitch might never get his hands dirty, but he certainly reaped the rewards of everyone else's hard work.

Bennett hated the controlling bastard. That hate, the anger that had ridden him so hard for so long, churned in his gut. Turning the key in the ignition, he backed out of the parking space and headed home, damning the entire Darcy clan along the way.

Every time he tangled with one of them, he felt raw. It was like they just peeled the skin right off him and left nothing but exposed nerves. He'd go home, have a beer, and beat the hell out of a heavy bag. It was the standard treatment whenever he had a Darcy run in. Even temporary relief was welcome.

When he reached his house, he grabbed the now warm six-pack of beer and headed inside, pausing only long enough to utilize the old bottle opener still mounted to the porch rail. As he stepped inside, he was greeted by seventy-five pounds of fur and slobber.

Bennett didn't get angry. He just slid to the floor right there inside the door while the dog laid against his chest and whined. Scratching his ears, Bennett sighed. *Big, dumb, drooling everywhere, and scared of flies, the dog was the best thing that had ever happened to him*, he thought.

"It's been a hell of a day, Slick," he muttered as the dog licked his cheek. "But I saw somebody you know."

The dog whined and cocked its head.

"That's just how I feel," Bennett replied and took another swig from the bottle. "That is just how I feel."

"Was she with him?"

Clayton Darcy met his father's gaze across the empty hospital waiting room and wondered, not for the first time, how cold the bastard really was. "Does it matter?"

Samuel Darcy narrowed his eyes at him. "Yes. I've told her—warned her—a dozen times about associating with the likes of him. All of the Hayes family is nothing but trouble, the lot of them!"

Clayton didn't bother to argue. He'd learned long ago that it did not a damn bit of good. "No. From what the sheriff told me, as best as it can be pieced together until Mia wakes up; she was driving on Fall Lick Road, rounded a bend, lost control of the vehicle and wound up in the creek. With the rain, it was deep enough to pull the car completely under. If he hadn't been there, we'd be at the morgue and not here."

"And a Hayes just happened to be right behind her?" Samuel summed up. His dubious tone clearly indicated how unlikely he found the tale.

"He does live on that road," Clayton pointed out. "Less than two miles from your house."

Samuel grimaced. "I'm well aware of that! I tolerated his grandmother because it was the decent thing to do, but if I'd known she was going to leave that house to him I might not have been so generous! I think he stayed here out of spite."

Probably, Clayton thought. Not for the first time, he enjoyed the notion. Bennett Hayes had made himself a thorn in Samuel Darcy's side and Clayton was ever so quietly cheering him on.

The conversation, if it could be called that, went no further. The doctor appeared, wearing scrubs and a white coat, a mask hanging around his neck.

"Mr. Darcy?"

"Yes," Samuel said. "How is my daughter?"

"Very lucky," the doctor stated. "She escaped a pretty catastrophic accident and her worst injury was a broken wrist. I'd say that borders on miraculous. We've set the bone and casted it. She's got a couple of stitches and she's still pretty out of it from the sedative we gave her. We'll be keeping her overnight but most likely she'll go home in the morning."

"Will she be scarred?" Samuel demanded. "We'll need a plastic surgeon consulted immediately, if that's likely."

The doctor blinked at him for a moment, and when he spoke again, his tone was perceptibly cooler. "The stitches are along the line of her eyebrow. Any scarring will be minimal, if not nonexistent. A few minor cuts and some very ugly bruises, but there's nothing she shouldn't make a full and unmarred recovery from."

Clayton rose. "Thank you, Doctor. When can we see her?"

The doctor spared another hard look for Samuel.

"Assuming she wants to see you? Once they've transported her from recovery to her room, you'll be able to visit with her."

Samuel sighed when he left. "At least she won't need surgery. Thank God."

Quentin snorted in disgust. "How about, 'thank God, she's all right' or 'thank God that bastard came along and fished her out of the creek before she drowned'? I don't like him any better than you do, but if he hadn't been there, she would have died and you're worried about her fucking looks?"

Samuel gifted his younger son with a cool look. "I am relieved that she will recover, of course. But that doesn't change the fact that Mia is the face of the distillery in many ways. She is in charge of our PR and marketing. How well do you think that would go if she were no longer beautiful? I suppose Erica could take over for her if it becomes necessary."

Clayton's temper flared. No one got under his skin quite like Samuel did. "Erica will not take over anything. In case you've forgotten, our agreement makes you little more than a figurehead at Fire Creek and your own recklessness has made you a financial liability. You don't make those kinds of decisions!"

"I am still your father, boy! You won't speak to me like that!" Samuel shouted. His voice was loud enough that several people in the hallway looked up in shock. Deciding on a different tactic, he turned the cajoling manipulation that was typically his first choice. "Just think what it would do to Mia if she had to see a scarred face in the mirror every day! Would you really want that for her?"

Disgusted with him, Clayton stated, "Mia will always be beautiful because it has nothing to do with her looks.

Now that you know she's okay, you should go. Quentin and I will stay with her."

"She's my daughter!" Samuel's reply was emphatic, but there wasn't a great deal of emotion behind it. With him, it was always a show.

"Really?" Clayton shot back. "Because from here it sounded more like you were talking about a corporate asset. You don't give a damn about any of us, and while Quentin and I are okay with that, she's still got a heart for you to break. So just go, old man."

Samuel pointed one finger at Clayton. "You're not in charge of the distillery just yet. Nothing is set in stone, boy! Mia will always side with me and without her that leaves you all at a paltry forty percent share."

Quentin rose then, getting up in his father's face. "Then take the damn distillery and stop holding it over our heads. You can't run the thing without us, anyway! You haven't put in an honest-to-god day's work in more than a decade and wouldn't know what to do even if we did step down. You've been too busy running around with two-bit whores half your age—hell, some of 'em are half my age!"

Samuel turned then to walk away, but as he reached the door to the small waiting area, he turned back to them. "You don't like me, you don't like the way I run things, you don't have to be around to witness it! I'll buy you out anytime."

"With what?" Clayton demanded. "We're keeping you afloat, in case you've forgotten! You've wasted the money you married Mama for!"

"Watch what you say to me, son," Samuel admonished. "And watch what you say about your mother!"

"All of a sudden you're the devoted husband? How long has it been since you even saw her?" Clayton demanded. "You've left Mia to rot in that house, wasting her life and her youth taking care of the woman you broke!"

Samuel lunged at him then, grasping Clayton's shirt collar. They were face to face, the older man breathing hard and Clayton with his fists clenched.

Quentin stepped between them. "Do not do this here. I'm not any happier with him than you are, Clay, but this kind of scene would be the last thing Mia...or Mama, would want!"

"Talk to me that way again, boy," Samuel warned. "Old as I am, I can still teach you a lesson."

"Any day." In spite of Clayton's deceptively calm facial expression, there was an edge to his voice that let no doubt he would relish the opportunity. "Any time."

Samuel shoved him away and turned toward the door.

Standing there, watching him walk away, Quentin turned to Clayton. "Did that really just happen? You, Mr. Always Cool, started a fucking screaming match with the old man in public?"

Clayton nodded. "Yep. I wish I'd hit him."

"You'd kill him. And while I don't have much use for him," Quentin added, "None of us want that. But since you put it all out there in the open, his financial woes and all, what the hell do we do now?"

"We go to work on Monday like always. Now let's go see our baby sister and figure out what the hell happened, then I'll head over to the house. Someone needs to stay with Mama tonight because it sure as hell won't be the philandering asshole she's married to."

"What the hell were you thinking?"

The voice on the phone was low and angry. The defensive response was automatic. "We needed her out of the way. Now she is."

"Out of the way does not equate attempted murder! Do I have to do everything my own damn self? Invite her out for a drink, be nice! Make friends! My lord, how did I raise someone so dumb? There were ways to get her out of that house that didn't involve trying to kill her."

The speaker's shrill voice prompted a wince. Nervously picking at her manicured nails, she snapped back, "Well, it's done now. And we might not get another opportunity, so you better find it and find it fast."

"On the contrary, even though you pulled an idiotic stunt, you did manage to do one thing right. There is no bigger distraction for Mia Darcy than Bennett Hayes. If her focus is on him, you could let off a stick of dynamite beside her and she wouldn't even notice!"

Her jaw dropped. "So, you're pissed at me for the accident even though it created just the kind of distraction you needed? That makes perfect fucking sense!"

Her mother's words, when she replied, were so clearly being uttered between clenched teeth that picturing her disapproving expression was easy. "Listen to me. No more going off script. No more winging it. When I give you an order, you will follow it. Right now, your job is to make Bennett Hayes believe that girl is in danger. As long as he does, he'll never leave her alone. That boy has a white knight complex if ever I've seen one. And as for Mia— well, who can resist a handsome man who wants to play the hero? Especially one that's forbidden. If people get hurt, then the police get involved. Neither one of us can afford that. Understood?"

The mention of police brought home just how disastrously wrong things could have gone. She was not cut out for prison. "Yes. I understand. Scare her. But don't hurt her. Send her running into his waiting arms. Right?"

"That about does it, and if you fuck this up, even though you are my only remaining child, I will hang you out to dry. You hear me?"

She smiled bitterly. Having never been her mother's favored child, she knew all too well how fleeting the woman's affections could be. "I never expected anything less from you, Mother."

Four

It was just after midnight when Bennett parked his truck and strode purposefully toward the hospital's entrance. The electronic doors under the red "Emergency Room" sign opened with a soft swoosh. The girl working behind the desk looked up, and recognizing him as the local lovelorn idiot, offered him a polite smile as she returned to her paperwork. He could feel the side-eye as he walked past and he wasn't even out of earshot when she started whispering to her coworker.

There was no denying that it was probably a huge mistake to come back. Clayton had called his aunt's house and left a message on her answering machine that Mia was okay, but that wasn't good enough. Bennett needed more than just okay.

He took the stairs up to the second floor. There were only two floors for the whole hospital and all of the patient rooms were up. At the nurse's station was a girl both he and Mia had gone to high school with.

"Hey, Stace," he greeted her. "I wanted to check on Mia."

She glanced up at him, clearly surprised and more than a little worried. "Bennett, I don't think that's a good idea."

"I pulled her out of that creek, Stacy. I ought to be able to find out how the hell she's doing," he replied, trying to keep his tone reasonable.

She bit her lip and gave a sideways glance at the other nurses who were on duty, all of whom pretended to be blissfully unaware of what was going on. "I can't tell you anything about her condition, but her family did sign a release to acknowledge that she's here and to allow visitors. Visiting hours are technically over, but if you wanted to come back tomorrow and see her, she's in room two-twenty-eight. It's just around the corner."

Bennett smiled at her. "You're a lifesaver, Stacy. Thank you."

"Don't thank me! Make your sister give me a big discount the next time I go to her store!"

He chuckled as he walked away. "Will do."

Around the corner and just out of sight of the nurse's station, he opened the door to Mia's room softly. He wanted to see her, to make certain for himself that she was okay, but if she was asleep, he'd leave her be.

The room was dark, save for the small amount of light that filtered in from the hallway. Approaching the bed, Bennett noted the bruises that marred her pale skin. They'd bloomed furiously in the hours since the accident, but he didn't doubt that over the next few days they'd get worse.

More tired than he'd been in a very long time, the events of the day finally catching up to him, he sank down onto the chair beside her bed.

It shouldn't have mattered so much. She should have been out of his system ages ago. But she wasn't, and he very much feared that she never would be. She'd dug in deep and there was no getting her out.

He cursed softly, but in the silence of the room, it was still enough to wake her. Her eyes fluttered open and she looked up, confused, disoriented, and then her gaze settled on him.

"Bennett?"

"I just came to make sure you were all right," he said. "Are you in pain?"

"A little, but I think it's more of a hangover than anything else," she replied, her speech slightly slurred.

He smiled. "I think driving your car over an embankment and into a creek might be contributing to that as much as the pain meds."

"I didn't," she said.

The hot clutch of fear was back. "Don't you remember?"

She gave him a look that clearly stated he was a moron. "Of course I remember. But there was another car there, Bennett. I swerved to miss them and when my car stopped, the back wheels were right there on the edge."

"So how'd you wind up in the creek then?"

"They pushed me," she replied calmly. "They drove their car right up to mine and pushed me over the edge."

The statement was made so matter-of-factly, that even as insane as it sounded, Bennett didn't dismiss it outright. "Are you sure about that?"

"Yes. I'm sure. Didn't you see them driving away?"

"No," he answered. The truth was that his attention had been on a break in the trees on the opposite side of the creek bank, just across the bridge. Anytime he was behind her on that road, he'd watch to see her driving around those hairpin turns at a speed that made him sweat. When he hadn't seen it, he'd known something was horribly wrong. "I just saw all the debris and the churned-up mud. I got out to look and saw your car sinking."

She shivered.

Noting her reaction, he offered. "Let's not talk about this now. I'll look into it."

"Swear to me. Don't just placate me because you think I'm drugged out of my mind!" she insisted.

"I promise."

A sad smile curved her lips. "And you always keep your promises."

"I didn't mean it like that," he said. "All that was a long time ago."

"Sometimes it feels like a lifetime."

He hadn't meant to bring up the past, though it was always present between them, a hovering ghost that gave neither of them any peace. Changing the subject, he focused on the here and now. "What kind of car was it?"

She frowned. "Big. Dark color. SUV. I don't know. I can't really think right now."

Bennett rose to his feet. On impulse, he leaned over and pressed a kiss to her forehead. It was an innocent gesture, utterly lacking in any carnal thought or intent. Even then, it was still electric. Touching her, being so close to her, it was salt in the wound.

"I'll let you know what I find." He stepped back from the hospital bed and headed for the door and the looming shadow of Clayton Darcy.

"I told you I'd let you know how she was," Clayton reminded him coolly.

Not in the mood to be taken to task, Bennett cocked an eyebrow at him. "Because a Darcy is as good as their word, right?"

"This is trouble—you are trouble for her." Clayton

made the statement dispassionately, as if matters were always that simple, that black and white.

"I'm not here for trouble. I needed to know she was okay and a secondhand account wasn't good enough. Just because I haven't knocked the shit out of you, doesn't mean I won't. I'm not a scrawny kid anymore and any advantage you had a decade ago is long gone now," Bennett replied firmly. He wasn't going to be bullied by them. The Darcy money and the Darcy name had kept him from the one thing he wanted most in life and he was done with it.

"I'm not threatening you, Bennett." Clayton kept his cool. His voice never rose and his expression remained calm. "I'm just stating the obvious. I know you loved her. I know she loved you. But neither one of you could have handled the shit storm that would have rained down on you if you'd been allowed to go through with your hare-brained plan."

"We'll never know. You and your worthless asshole of a father made sure of that."

"I asked you to leave that night," Clayton said, "and when you wouldn't, I made you leave. If I hadn't, Samuel would have put a bullet in you. Mia didn't need that. She'd lost enough already."

Bennett sneered at him. "Am I supposed to thank you for that?"

Clayton moved toward him. "You were kids who thought you could live on love. You had no job, no prospects, no way to support her. Mia's never known poverty. Did you really want to be the dickhead who not only introduced her to it but forced her to live in it?"

That statement echoed the doubts and recriminations that Bennett had battled for the last ten years. He met Clayton's questioning gaze directly, his jaw clenched and fists tight. He hated having the smug fucker in his head. "Is there a point to this conversation or are you just gonna keep wasting my time?"

Clayton cocked his head to one side and then said simply, "You're not a broke kid anymore, and Mia's not a wide-eyed little girl. So what the hell is stopping you now?"

Bennett didn't have an answer for that. Habit. Fear. Resignation. There were a dozen excuses, but not a one of them was *enough*. "You and I both know Samuel would never let it stand."

Clayton shoved his hands in his pockets and rocked back on his heels. "If you want her, go after her, and leave Samuel to me."

"What kind of game are you playing?" Bennett demanded. The swirling mix of anger and hope inside him left him reeling, unsteady. It wasn't a feeling he liked.

"No games. I've only ever done what I thought was best for her. That'll never change."

Bennett didn't say anything else as Clayton moved past him and into Mia's hospital room. Of course, he didn't need to. Clayton had dropped the bomb and walked away.

"Goddamn the Darcys," he muttered as he made his way toward the stairs. He needed out, he needed to think, and above all, he needed to figure out if he was willing to take the risk of letting Mia rip his heart out again.

As Bennett left the hospital, his mind was preoccupied with the conversation that had just taken place with Clayton, and honestly, with Mia. She was always taking up space in his mind, whether he wanted to admit it or not. He didn't believe in ghosts, but he sure as hell believed in hauntings. There was no other way to describe how she made him feel.

Focused on her, on the turmoil that was churning inside him and eating him up, he didn't notice the dark SUV parked at the back of the parking lot, partially in shadow and all but invisible in the night.

Climbing behind the wheel of his truck, Bennett headed for his house, the lonely solace of the big bed he'd be sleeping in alone. Except for Slick, he thought with a smile. The dog would be there, snoring and farting all night, whether he liked it or not.

Easing the truck onto the road, he was nearly at the end of the street before the black SUV pulled out of the hospital parking lot and followed him at a distance.

Five

Bennett stared at the tire tracks in the dirt and frowned. Even with all the rain, there was enough left for him to worry. It wasn't the churned-up mess from under the wheels of Mia's car that bothered him. It was the lone tread of a much larger vehicle right over top of the tracks left by her car that didn't quite mesh with the single car theory. Those tracks were much more in line with what she'd said at the hospital the night before.

There was a chance, he reminded himself, that the tracks were due to the scene being contaminated. The only thing he was an expert at was building furniture, but common sense wasn't too difficult to apply. He'd parked his truck on the side of the road. The EMTs, when they'd finally arrived, had been in the middle of the road. It was still possible some idiot curiosity seeker in a pickup or SUV had driven right up to the edge to look over at the submerged sports car.

It wasn't just the tracks. There were other things as well. Even though the accident scene had been cleaned, there were still bits of busted plastic and acrylic ground into the asphalt. Since it was considered to be a single car accident, just what could she have connected with in the middle of the roadway?

The sound of an approaching vehicle brought him to his feet, but he relaxed instantly when he saw the battered pickup. His cousin Carter had been 'fixing it up' for years, only nothing ever got fixed. Just patched. The muffler had more holes in it than a sieve.

"That damn thing will outlive us all," Bennett said as Carter parked the vehicle and stepped out.

"What the hell are you doing, man?" Carter demanded. His shaggy dark hair was scraped back into a ponytail and the thermal undershirt he wore was streaked with grease.

Bennet shrugged. "I just feel like there's more to this than meets the eye."

"She's fucking with your head again, Bennett!"

Bennett ignored the anger that statement prompted and focused on the words themselves. "*She* is in the hospital and very nearly died yesterday. The only thing she's doing is sleeping off pain meds. I'm out here by my own choice."

Carter shook his head. "Did she ask you to do this?"

Bennett didn't answer, but his hard glare was apparently telling enough.

"I knew it!" Carter said. "She batted her eyelashes and here you are, her errand boy, all over again!"

"She asked me to look into the accident because she believed another car was present! Should I have told her no?" Bennett demanded. He wasn't angry. Just frustrated and tired of everyone in town watching the two of them like hawks. Assholes and opinions, everybody had them.

Carter raised his hands. "You can get as mad as you

want to, but the truth of the matter is, Bennett, that girl ties you up in damn knots. She always has and she always will. But if you decide to get tangled up with her again, that's on nobody but you!"

"You're damn right. My business, my decision."

Carter made to walk away, heading for his truck. "Don't come crying to me when she dumps your ass again, not unless you plan on buying the beer!"

Bennett shook his head. "Before you go off pouting like a two-year-old, I need you to take a look at this."

Carter strolled back over and stared down at the pavement for a split second. "Don't see a damn thing."

"Dammit, Carter! Look at the broken plastic from the headlights! How did the rear end of her car go through the guardrail and the front lights get smashed in the same spot in a single car accident?"

Carter stopped and put his hands on his hips as he considered the question. "It's impossible. The only way that could have happened is if there was another vehicle or something else to strike the front end. Do you really believe that? There's no proof that this is debris from her accident."

Bennett stooped down and brushed his fingers over the pavement, picking up fragments of the plastic. "This road was resurfaced a month ago and there haven't been any accidents in this location other than Mia's. I went back to the hospital last night to check on her. She told me that there was another car—a black SUV with a deer guard. What if it wasn't an accident? What if they deliberately pushed her over?"

Carter shook his head. "You're reaching...you're reaching because you want a reason to bring her back into your life."

"No, I'm not. But if someone is trying to hurt her, I can't ignore it," Bennett argued.

"Sure you can. She's ignored you for ten years."

Bennett sighed and rose to his feet. "You don't pull any punches, do you? Ever?"

Carter leaned against his truck and crossed his arms over his chest. "That woman turned you inside out and you haven't been right since. You think I shouldn't ask questions after you played hero and ran off to the hospital like you're some lovesick Romeo? I might not have made the best grades in school, but even I know that shit didn't end well!"

Bennett's lips firmed and his gaze hardened. "I can handle this."

"I hope so," Carter said. As he climbed into his truck, he turned around and looked back. "Tread carefully."

Bennett watched him drive away and cursed under his breath. He wasn't foolish enough to completely disregard Carter's warnings. Mia got to him, she got inside his head like no one else ever had. But if she was in danger, he'd do whatever it took to protect her.

Staring down at the tiny shards of busted glass and plastic, Bennett cursed. It felt good so he said it again, louder. "Fuck my life."

It had been two days since the accident. Mia had spent the first day after being released from the hospital dealing with her mother. Patricia's condition never really changed. Every neurologist, every specialist, had a different opinion of just how aware Patricia was of what was happening around her. Mia had her own theories about that. Patricia couldn't respond, yet whenever there was turmoil or upheaval in the family, her mother would always have some sort of physical reaction. Seizures, blood pressure spikes, something would happen. Mia's accident was no different. Since then, Patricia had been having mild seizures with much greater frequency. Whether it was the bruises, the cast, she felt like her mother could see something in her present battered appearance that was upsetting to her.

She was having to face the very real fact that until she was healed, someone else would have to care for her mother. It was causing more harm than good for her to be around her mother at the moment. There was only one course of action and that was to hire someone to help with Patricia's care for the time being. In the interim, her soon-to-be former sister-in-law was helping out.

To save her sanity, Mia had left the house. She hadn't had a plan to start out with, but it didn't really surprise her where she'd wound up. As much as the accident had been on her mind, her rescuer had taken up residence there as well. Bennett was just as dangerous to her as the accident had been.

She'd cut through the woods, taking a path that was suspiciously well worn. It brought her out just to the right of Bennett's house. She had a dozen reasons to turn around and just head back home, but not a one of them trumped the undeniable fact that you didn't let something as monumental as someone literally saving your life pass without acknowledgment. There was another tiny, traitorous part of her that whispered insidiously in her mind that any excuse to see him was worthwhile.

As she emerged from the dense tree cover, she could hear the sound of power tools and the low wail of country music coming from behind the house. Rather than knock on the door, she followed the noise.

The double doors of the old barn turned workshop were wide open and she could see Bennett standing at his table cutting pieces of trim. He wore a plaid shirt, the buttons undone and hanging open over jeans so old and faded it was a wonder they didn't just disintegrate into nothing.

She noted the pieces he was working on, the intricately carved molding and trim work undoubtedly rescued from some dilapidated house. In the middle of the workroom was a large piano, keys missing, the entirety of it painted an unlikely shade of blue. She had no idea what it would be transformed into, but she silently acknowledged that his little sister, Savannah Hayes, and the store she'd created, Revision, were a raging success. Repurposed vintage and antiques along with fantastic architectural salvage had put them on the map and Bennett played a big part in that.

He must have sensed her presence. While she was still standing there drinking in the sight of him, the power tool he'd been working with had been switched off. Only the low hum of music from the docking station filled the space. Glancing up from the broad and rippling expanse of his chest, she met his gaze and blushed.

Silence stretched between them, taut and expectant. There were so many things that needed to be said, but most of them wouldn't make a difference, she thought sadly. They were stuck on the course she'd chosen. Even though just looking at him set her heart racing, and being so close to him made her want things with a kind of desperation she'd all but forgotten, she couldn't afford to let those things matter.

Finally, to break the fragile quiet, she said, "I should have called but I didn't have your number."

He removed his safety glasses and set them aside. "Why are you here, Mia?"

She hesitated for a moment, uncertain of how to begin. She had questions and he was the only one who could give her answers. "I need to talk to you about the accident."

He sighed and then scrubbed his hands over his face. "Let's go inside. I could use a drink for this."

Mia followed him up the steps of the back porch and through the back door. The kitchen was spotless, more from lack of use than his incredible housekeeping skills, or at least she assumed so. He reached up and grabbed two glasses from the cabinet and then pulled down a bottle. She recognized the label immediately. It was theirs.

"I'm surprised you'd have that in here," she remarked.

"I might not have much use for your family, but they make damn fine bourbon," he said as he poured a couple of fingers in each glass.

Their conversation was interrupted by the sound of nails clicking on the hardwood floor. They increased in speed until the dog came hurtling into the kitchen, sliding every which way on the linoleum until it ended up in a heap at her feet.

Looking down at the dark head and floppy ears, she felt tears stinging her eyes. "Slick? But, I thought...Daddy sent him to the shelter."

"I liberated him," he said.

"How?" she demanded.

He just shook his head. "Someone told me what had happened and...well, you know I always loved that dog."

Mia smiled as she kneeled down and nuzzled the dog, burying her face against his thick neck. He was older, the fur around his muzzle white with age, but god, it felt good to see him. He licked her hands, her face, whatever he could reach, clearly ecstatic to be with her again. "Oh, I have missed you so," she said softly. The dog whined back at her.

"Looks like the feeling is mutual."

Mia rose but kept her hand on the dog's head, rubbing his soft ears while he leaned against her leg and panted happily. It took her a minute to be able to utter the words, to force them past the lump in her throat. God above, the man made her insane. How could anyone be that good, that selfless? "Thank you for taking him, Bennett, for taking care of him."

He was clearly uncomfortable with the praise, so he handed her the glass and changed the subject. "So what do you want to know?"

She took a deep breath. When that didn't work to calm her nerves, she took a sip of the amber liquid. There was no burn. It was smooth and sweet on her tongue.

"Did you see anyone at the scene? Any other vehicles?" she asked.

"No. I drove up and saw the churned-up mud and broken light covers where you hit the guardrail. If it hadn't been for that—" He stopped to take a sip of his own whiskey. When he continued, his voice was deeper, gruffer. "You drive too fast, Mia. You always have. You hit that curve like a bat out of hell. If I hadn't come along, hadn't realized you'd been on that road right in front of me, you would have died there."

Her blood ran cold. He said it so matter-of-factly. It was true. She knew that. But it didn't change the fact that she hadn't been alone on that road, and her car hadn't gone into the creek without someone else forcing her over the edge. "I do drive too fast, but I only swerved and lost control because of the other car, Bennett!"

"I know," he said softly.

"It was a big black SUV. I'm not really sure what kind. With all those bars on the front of it," she continued on, not quite processing that he'd agreed with her.

"The deer guard." The words were supplied in an even tone, no censure, not disbelief.

"Yes," she replied adamantly. "I rounded the bend and it was parked in a way that it blocked both lanes!"

"I believe you," he said. "You don't have to convince me that it happened that way."

She stopped then, drew a deep breath and stared at him in stunned disbelief. "You believe me?"

"Yes. I saw the glass and plastic where your headlights got busted in. Directly in line with where your back wheels went over the edge. It's not possible for you to have simultaneously damaged the front and back end of your car in a single car accident before the rollover."

"It was deliberate," she said softly.

"Maybe they just panicked," he offered.

"I need another drink," she said.

Bennett refilled her glass.

"Someone tried to kill me, Bennett," she stated it emphatically. "I'm not imagining that. They waited for me on that road!"

"Why would someone do that, Mia? No one has any reason to hate you that badly," he shot back before draining his glass.

"You do," she finished quietly.

His eyes widened for a second in surprise, before narrowing in anger. "You come into my fucking house and accuse me of something like that?"

She shook her head. "No. I wasn't accusing you. I

know you'd never do anything like that. But it's true, Bennett...you do have every reason to hate me."

He settled back against the counter, arms crossed over his chest, muscles rippling and bunching beneath the open plaid shirt. "I don't hate you, Mia. I've tried to. I've tried to, every damn day of my life, and I just can't."

She set her glass on the counter. Her hand was trembling too much to hold on to it. "Do you need to hate me, Bennett? Clearly whatever was between us hasn't kept you from having a very active love life!"

He leaned his head back against the cabinet door and stared up at the ceiling as if praying for strength, or possibly patience. "That's not how it works. I wasn't the one who stood you up."

She glanced beyond the kitchen and into the living room, where new and decidedly feminine curtains hung over the window behind the couch. "It looks like you've managed okay. You and Lacey."

His eyebrow shot up. "You really wanna go there? We haven't been together for ten years! Should I have waited, Mia?"

"No," she said quickly. "And I didn't mean it like that, Bennett! Shit. Yes, I did, but I know I don't have the right. I'm jealous and not just because you're with someone else, but because you've made a life for yourself. And I'm still doing the same thing I was at eighteen. Taking care of Mama, handling the distillery tours and—" She stopped speaking abruptly, the unfinished words hanging between them.

The silence was heavy, laden with the anticipation of what went unsaid between them, the tension building until it was unbearable. It was Bennett who finally snapped. "And what, Mia? For the love of God, just say it!"

"And thinking about you. All the time," she replied. "At this point, I should be nothing more than a distant memory to you, and you're on my mind all the time."

He smiled, but there was no humor in it. It was a bitter and self-deprecating twist of his beautiful mouth. "Not so distant. I see you in town. I see your car speeding up and down this road. I hear your name whispered by every gossip in town as I walk past them. People in this town remember everything. They remember us. And so do I."

She had memories of her own. His mouth on hers, his hands on her body. They'd been greedy then with the newness of it all, just a couple of inexperienced kids with more hormones than skill. Of course, Bennett was more experienced now, but more than that, the heat that burned between them then was still there. Dating wasn't a part of her life. There was no time for it. Taking care of her mother and her job at the distillery, it was almost like time had stopped for her that summer. He'd gone on with his life, at least somewhat, and she was in the same rut she'd always been in.

She'd made a glaring mistake in coming here and it was staring her right in the face. Panic hit, sinking into her gut like a twisting knife. Seeing him, being close enough to him to smell him, to touch him, it was an epic error in judgment on her part. Nothing in this world could hurt her as much as the man in front of her. The first time had been bad enough. To go through it all again when the outcome couldn't be any different was just more than she could contemplate. "I should go," she managed, "coming here was a mistake."

She whirled and headed for the door and was halfway there when he caught her. One of his large hands snaked out and captured her undamaged wrist, closing over it and tugging her back to him. "You're right. I know you're right, and I don't fucking care."

With her chest close to his, her head just below his chin, his arms slid around her. It was like breathing, the most natural thing in the world. She leaned into him, savoring the heat, the hard press of him against her. "I cannot even count the number of ways in which this is a bad idea. There's no way this ends well, Bennett."

"Never say never," he advised softly.

"Highly unlikely, then," she amended.

"Lots of things are unlikely, O wise one. Doesn't mean they can't happen." His voice was little more than a deep murmur, his lips brushing against her forehead as he spoke. He held her gently, tenderly. It was something she'd missed so much it wasn't even possible to put into words. Even then, the heat was there, arcing between them, taking on a life of its own.

"Like what?" she asked. Her skin burned beneath his hand like he'd set her on fire. With nothing more than a touch, it raged for him.

"You standing here in my kitchen, for starters."

"I'm blaming my lapse in judgment on painkillers." The statement was flippant, but the quavering of her voice and the slight hitch in her breathing told the truth. There was nothing casual about what was happening between them. It was life or death.

"Why is it a mistake?" he demanded as he pulled her a little closer to him.

All the reasons fled along with the fear. With the heat of his body against hers, his breath warm on her skin, she couldn't pull them to mind anymore. She could see the fine sheen of sweat on his skin from where he'd been working. Her breath caught as she looked up. His eyes weren't locked on hers. Instead, they were locked on her mouth. He looked at her lips as if he wanted to bite into her and in that moment, she would have let him.

"Mia," he murmured. It was the last thing that was said between them. He descended upon her, his lips on hers as his hands slid upward to tangle in the fall of her hair.

It was a gentle kiss. She didn't doubt for a moment that Bennett was aware of every injury and mindful not to hurt her. That was just who he was. But as his mouth moved over hers in a kiss that was achingly tender, her body burned for him. When he captured her bottom lip between his, she melted against him. His arms closed around her, pulling her even closer until she was firmly pressed against the hard wall of his chest. She could feel him everywhere.

Then his hands slid downward, cupping her behind, pressing their bodies even more tightly together. The blatant evidence of his desire was unmistakable and her body responded to it insistently. She wanted him. She wanted him with a desperation that she couldn't even articulate.

The dog whined then, butting his large head between them and demanding to be given the lion's share of the attention. Breathless, aching, desperate, and more than a little embarrassed that she'd fallen so easily into Bennett's arms, Mia backed away from him.

"What are we doing, Bennett?" The question was anguished, reflecting the war that raged inside her between the desire to have what she wanted and the need to do what was best for everyone.

"We're doing what we want for a change," he replied. "I don't know why you bailed on me that night. I may never know, but there's one thing I'm sure of, Mia."

"What's that?"

"Whatever your reason for not showing up," he said firmly. "It wasn't because you don't want me—because you don't want *us*."

Forcing herself to move away from him completely, Mia disentangled herself from his arms. She couldn't think clearly when he touched her, obviously. "Wanting something doesn't mean you should have it."

"That's a fine rule for children. It doesn't fly with me. I'm a grown man, and God knows you're a grown woman. Nobody, Mia, and I mean nobody, ought to have a say in what happens between us except us."

"I have to go," she said, fighting down feelings of panic all the while fighting the urge to just throw herself at him.

He smiled, that slow and lazy grin spreading over his beautiful lips. "That's fine. I don't think you're up for what I have in mind, anyway. But mark my words, when you're well, when the scrapes and bruises have healed, we're revisiting this, Mia."

"What about Lacey?" she demanded, flinging the only ammunition at him that she had.

His smile shifted, becoming more self-deprecating than amused. "Lacey and I haven't been seeing each other for months now. You're behind on your gossip."

Her lips parted on a surprised 'O.' "You broke up with her?"

He shook his head. "No. She dumped me. I gave her a ring and she said she didn't want to spend her life with a man who would always wish she was someone else. Second time in my life I've bought a ring for a woman and wound up keeping it."

It was like a punch in the gut, that reminder of what they could have had together. "I have to go, Bennett. I can't be here with you...I can't think."

With that, Mia turned and fled, retreating to the small path through the woods. She left him behind, along with her beloved pet that he'd rescued and the last vestiges of hope she'd had that one day, she'd be over him for good. Bennett Hayes was a part of her, and he always would be. It would haunt her forever.

Six

Bennett leaned against the doorframe and watched her go. He'd pushed and she'd run. There was nothing new in that sequence of events, he thought bitterly.

The thought had no sooner crossed his mind than he heard the sound of the front screen door slamming. It would be Carter, of course. He considered knocking to be an inefficient use of his time, or perhaps he was just so certain of his welcome it never occurred to him that he ought to check.

"Dude, what the fuck?" His cousin's query, without preamble or tact, was typical.

"Mind your own business, Carter," Bennett said without turning around.

"I figured I was allowed to have an opinion," Carter groused. "Or at the very least a good reason to bust your balls."

"You figured wrong," Bennett said, pouring another finger of the bourbon in his glass. "I can handle this."

Carter laughed—hard. He bent over double with his

hands on his knees and laughed until he couldn't breathe. Bennett just glared at him as he sipped the amber liquid.

Finally, breathless and wiping tears from his eyes, Carter rose to his full height and shook his head. "You're so damn dumb, I almost feel sorry for you."

Bennett poured another glass of bourbon and handed it to his overly opinionated cousin. "I get that you don't have more than a passing acquaintance with sympathy, Carter, but in general, people don't express it by laughing so hard they damn near piss themselves."

"Can't help it," Carter replied, taking the glass and slamming the bourbon before handing it back for a refill. "You do realize this is the gust of wind that stirs the shit storm, right?"

Truer words had never been spoken. The feud between their families had gone on for almost a century. Once upon a time, his great-grandfather had been a business partner to Mia's. They'd started Fire Creek Distillery together but when William Hayes died, his heirs had been unable to produce the documents to show that he'd had part ownership and Thomas Allen Darcy had been less than forthcoming. He'd denied any claim the Hayes family had on the distillery and had instead claimed that William had been nothing more than a trusted employee and friend.

The whole town of Fontaine had known it was a lie, but no one was willing to speak out against Darcy, just like no one in the present day was willing to speak out against Samuel. With Mia and her mother being the only exceptions, there wasn't a single Darcy that he would piss on if they were on fire.

"You've made your point. Why are you here?" Bennett demanded.

Carter shrugged. "Emmitt's tearing down that old

barn today, figured a little destruction might improve your mood."

"You're driving," Bennett said as he moved toward the door. "You've had less bourbon."

He climbed into the passenger seat of Carter's beat-up truck. Something was jabbing his hip and he fished around in the seat until he produced a high-heeled shoe. He held it up just as Carter climbed behind the wheel. "Changing up your wardrobe a little?"

Carter laughed. "She said she lost that in here. I thought she made it up to have an excuse to come back!"

"Who?"

Carter raised an eyebrow. "Like I'm gonna tell!"

Bennett knew that Carter was a player, but to his knowledge, Carter never promised any woman more than a good time. "So you can butt your big ass nose into my business but I'm not allowed to know yours?"

Carter took the shoe and tossed it behind the seat. "That's not 'business.' That was one wild, crazy and truly fantastic night that will never be repeated. No harm, no foul. This thing with you and Mia is going to bring hell down on all of us. You know that, right?"

Bennett sighed. "I know."

For the longest time, they sat there in silence until Carter finally turned the key in the ignition. "Is she worth it?"

"A million times over," Bennett admitted.

"Then do what you gotta do and we'll sort out the mess later."

Mia made the climb back up the hill a lot slower than the trip down had been. Part of that was physical. Her body hurt and fighting gravity wasn't exactly a good option for her at the moment. The second was a little more complicated. She didn't want to go home. Part of her was still lingering in Bennett's kitchen, savoring the slow-building heat that flared between them, the hard press of his body against hers.

When she walked back into her house, she wouldn't be hot, sexy Mia anymore. She'd be Mia the caregiver. It would be conversations about her mother's feeding, about her intake and output, about seizures and repositioning her and any signs of bedsores or skin breakdowns. Sometimes, Mia felt lost in it, like the pieces that made her a person in her own right just vanished into all those details.

She wanted to hang onto that for just a little bit longer, that feeling of being wanted, of being desired, of being something *more*.

"You cannot get sucked back into this," she whispered aloud. "There's no good way for it to end."

At the sharp snap of a twig, Mia's head swung around. She winced in pain, but managed to keep quiet as she listened for any indication of movement.

Coyotes had become a menace and if it was just one, it would probably be more terrified of her than she of it, but if there was more than one, she could be in a lot of trouble.

Another snap and her breath caught. But then the woods went completely still. No birds, no rustling of leaves, nothing. It was dead quiet. Fear hit her then, hard. It settled in her gut and set her heart pounding.

Mia didn't wait to see who was there, she didn't wait to see who might come through the trees. She just ran.

Turning on her heels, she moved as fast as her battered body would allow.

She was nearing the edge of the woods when she became aware of thrashing sounds behind her. Looking back wasn't an option. It would slow her down and she couldn't afford that.

As she broke through the trees into her own backyard, she saw Annalee sitting on the porch. The woods behind her had gone quiet again. Risking it, she glanced over her shoulder. The foliage was so dense it was almost impossible to see anything. Even as the thought occurred, she saw something; a dark, hulking shape moved, slinking deeper into the woods.

"What the hell spooked you so bad?" Annalee demanded.

Mia turned and faced her former sister-in-law. It was the strangest thing that she was the one Clayton had turned to for help, but it all made sense. She knew Patricia, her moods, her needs, and for whatever reason, in spite of their very acrimonious split, she'd agreed to help out.

"I'm just jumpy, I think," Mia offered.

"I know what's at the bottom of that path, Mia. It's your own guilty conscience that's got you on the run," Annalee offered sagely.

"I've nothing to feel guilty about. Who I see and when I see them is nobody's business but mine," Mia shot back angrily.

Annalee cocked an eyebrow. "Ooh! Rebellion! I've never seen this side of you, Mia. You ought to let it out more often. You see who you want, you do what you want. You've been doing it for everyone else far too long anyway."

Mia shook her head as she moved past Annalee toward

the door. "I'm gonna take a long hot bath. I was sore enough to begin with but running through the woods like a fool sure can't help."

"You do that, honey. I told Clay that I'd stay the night and look after Patricia."

Mia had to ask, "Why are you two all of a sudden getting along so well? Two months ago, you couldn't be in the same room without drawing blood!"

Annalee shook her head. "You keep your secrets, Mia. I'll keep mine."

Seven

ia was at her desk, reviewing the handful of applications she'd received after advertising for a caregiver for her mother. The follow-up visit with the orthopedist the day before had not been good news. The cast would have to stay on for at least six weeks and then there would be physical therapy afterward. There was a very real possibility that it could be months before she could do all the necessary tasks related to her mother's care.

It was not what she had wanted to hear. If there was one bright spot, the applicants did at least look promising. Hiring a second caregiver to work in the evenings, in addition to the one that worked days while she was at the distillery, would cut into her savings. It was useless asking her father for money. He would offer all sorts of helpful solutions about how she could economize while he was making dinner reservations for his Barbie du jour.

The knock on her door pulled her back to the present and she glanced up to see Clayton hovering in the doorway. "You got a minute?" he asked.

"Sure. What's up?" she asked as she set aside the folder.

"What's all this?"

"I've got to hire someone else to help with Mama. At least short term," she admitted reluctantly. It bothered her that she was having to depend on others to do what she'd always done for her mother. But changing and cleaning feeding tubes, dealing with the seizures that still plagued her at times, cleaning her up, changing her, repositioning her, those were all things that required two hands and Mia just didn't have them at the moment.

"That's good. You should have hired someone a long time ago."

"I can take care of Mama...most of the time."

Clayton sighed. "I'm not saying you can't. I'm just saying that you don't always take care of you. Having help, having a moment to yourself, that doesn't make you a bad daughter. And it doesn't mean you don't work your ass off to take care of her."

Mia shrugged. "I know all that. When I need help, I ask for it."

"No," he replied. "You don't. You get quiet. You withdraw. You retreat so far into yourself that it seems like you're going to disappear."

The truth of those words peeled back the layers of her day-to-day existence and left her feeling exposed in a way that she resented. "Seeing a therapist, Clayton, doesn't make you one. I can handle things on my own."

He held up his hands. "I didn't come to fight. I just wanted to let you know that I've had a talk with Erica and the proposal is dead in the water. Not happening. Will never happen. She knows that."

Mia settled back in her chair. "That's good. Thank you. How solvent are we, Clay? Be honest."

"We're okay. Assuming Samuel doesn't buy new boobs for his latest girlfriend, or a house, or a car."

"He'd better not buy that bitch a car," Mia said.

"That bitch is apparently no longer dating our father, or if she is, she's not the only one. He's moved out of her condo for greener and probably younger pastures."

Mia grimaced. "Of course he did. Okay, so the money. Tell me."

Settling onto the edge of the desk, he answered carefully, each word well considered. "The distillery is making money. The proceeds from the orders we were able to fill have begun to roll in. Doing a limited number of preorders for the next batch has kept our cash trickling, if not flowing. With the scaled back salaries for all of us, the next quarter will be good. Why?"

"Because we need to do something big. If we want to be competitive with the larger, and more well-known and better branded distilleries, then we need to put ourselves out there. I think we should do a sponsorship with Keenland. The world of thoroughbred racing is synonymous with luxury and that's what we need to be. There are a few spots in April that could work for us."

He whistled through his teeth. "The Spring meet?"

"Yes. They've sent me the information I requested and I've looked at the numbers. It's a big chunk of our marketing budget for the year, but I think the potential benefits would make it worthwhile. A corporate sponsorship this year and next, building to sponsoring a small stakes race in the next five. Who knows? Eventually the name Fire Creek could be attached to a Derby, or heaven help us, a Triple Crown winner." Establishing an affiliation between Fire Creek and what was essentially the debutante ball for any horse worth knowing about in the racing world could be huge for them.

Mia was in her comfort zone talking about the distillery, about how to make it bigger, better, more successful. That and her mother were the extent of her life. If that thought made her a little sad, so be it. "I've also made the arrangements for our spot at the Bourbon Festival. We'll have a booth at the Equestrian Games, as well. Branding Fire Creek as a luxury item and targeting that market is a big step in the right direction."

"Send me the proposal and if we can make it work, and if Quentin is in agreement, we'll make it happen," he offered. Changing the subject, he tapped on the applications. "Have you talked to anyone yet?"

"I had one interview earlier this morning. She was a no. I've got someone else coming in at three. On paper, she's perfect. I checked her references already and they're solid. Was a nurse before, though her license has expired. Married a doctor. Divorced said doctor, and I can't but feel like I know her. The name is very familiar. If her personality clicks, I'll probably hire her immediately. I don't have a lot of time to spare. Annalee has been incredibly helpful, but it can't be easy on her, or you."

"Annalee and I have an understanding," he said. "We're good."

"It hurts, doesn't it?"

"Yes. But so do lots of things. It won't kill me."

Mia looked at her brother, really looked at him. He was working himself to the bone, and it wasn't just the distillery. Clayton always played things close to the vest and she knew there was more going on. "What's really going on in your head, Clay? If you'd tell me, I'd help you."

"I can't. It's not that I don't want to or that I don't trust you. I don't know what I'm looking for yet, Mia, but when I find it, it will change everything."

"This is about Samuel, isn't it?"

Clayton sighed. "I've got to find a way to get his hands out of the pot, Mia. If we don't, we're always going to be struggling to keep the business afloat."

"And Annalee, does she know?" Mia asked.

"Yes. Of course," he said sarcastically. "Why on earth would I put this ugliness on her, after everything else?"

Mia shook her head. "Lord, you are dumb. I love you so much, Clay, but sometimes I forget that you are a man and prone to masculine idiocy. She loves you! Still. And you're pissing it away!"

Staring out the window of her office that overlooked the storehouse where every precious barrel was aging and waiting its turn, he said, "The distillery, the constant fighting with Samuel for control, of trying to curb his insane spending, it took a toll. She wanted things I couldn't give her."

Wouldn't. The word was in her mind, but she didn't utter it. Clayton, under his typically mild-mannered exterior, could be as proud and stubborn as the rest of them. "I'm sorry."

"What about you and Hayes? He's still got it bad for you. And it's pretty clear you're in the same boat. This—hiring someone to help with Mama—Mia, this is your chance to live a little."

Her heart literally skipped a beat at the thought. But she quickly squashed that little flare of hope. There were things Clayton didn't know, and she could never tell him. If she did, it would tear the whole family apart. "You're not suggesting that I attempt to rekindle my relationship with Bennett? Do I need to tell you how much of a disaster that would be?"

"I didn't say you had to walk down Main Street holding his hand. You're a goddamn adult, Mia."

"My big brother is encouraging me to have a scandalous affair. As if our father isn't bad enough, you've got to bring this Jerry Springer moment to my door?" she hedged.

"I'm just putting it out there. Live your life. Be as discreet or indiscreet about it as you choose. Self-denial is cold comfort." Clayton rose and turned toward the door, but paused to look back at her. "If you could have anything you wanted, Mia, what would it be?"

Bennett. She didn't say it. She didn't have to. If the world were different, if her life was something other than what it was, they'd be married, maybe even have babies. That thought cut like a knife and she pushed it back, locked it down like she always did. "I can't. So there's no point thinking about it."

"Take a risk, Mia. Before it's too late, take a damn risk."

When he'd gone, Mia sank back in her chair, the weight of everything pressing in on her. The car crash, whoever had been following her through the woods, Erica's scheming to get into Samuel's good graces, Samuel's clear loss of interest in Erica, Clayton's assertion that Samuel had now thrown over the former beauty queen for another, caring for her mother, Clayton's looming divorce and Quentin, well, she didn't know what the hell was going on with Quentin. In the midst of all of that, she couldn't afford the added drama of an affair with Bennett. But still, it tempted her, it tempted her strongly.

Memories long buried stirred to life, of him sneaking into her bedroom in the dark of night, of hot, drugging kisses in the back seat of his daddy's car. She wanted him as much as she ever had, but she'd made a deal with the devil, or in her case, a deal with her father. If he found out, everything would come crashing down around her.

"So don't let him find out," she whispered to the empty room.

A frisson of excitement burned through her at the thought. Just for a little while, she'd get to live again.

Eight

Bennett put down the planer and ran his hand over the wood. The doors on the old cabinet were being stubborn, but finally, after about a million small adjustments, they were closed and flush to the base.

"There," he said and pointed to the near perfect seam. "That, little sister, is craftsmanship."

"That, big brother, took you almost the whole day," Savannah replied smartly, flipping her blonde hair over her shoulder. "Your head isn't in the game today, Bennett."

That was certainly true. He'd forgotten half his tools at home and had to go back for them. Then he'd mixed up the addresses for deliveries and sent Carter to the wrong house. Sleep had been in short supply. It had been two days since the scene in his kitchen with Mia, two days and she was still wreaking havoc on him.

Thinking about Mia and about whether or not she really was in danger from someone, had kept him awake. A part of him wanted to dismiss the accident as just a fluke or aberration. But his gut wouldn't let him. It didn't feel right to him. Or maybe it was wishful thinking on his part. Maybe, he thought, he just wanted her to need him.

"Everyone has an off day," he replied to Savannah.

"Umm hmm." It was a noncommittal response murmured as she quickly drew out a design in her always-present sketchbook.

Bennett shook his head. She'd been all set to poke into his business and then got distracted by her own designs. It was typical Savannah.

"I'm taking off early," he said, packing up his tools.

"Drop off those two ladder-back chairs to Ruby Thompson? She wants them for her Christmas display this year."

Bennett nodded his agreement as he headed out the door. With his tools stowed in the front, he put the chairs in the back and secured them with bungee cords. Just as he was tightening the last one, he felt a prickle of unease. Glancing across the street, it was impossible to miss the black SUV with the deer guard.

Casually, Bennett started across the street, ready to confront them. Before he'd even crossed the first lane of the street, the engine roared to life and the SUV peeled out. Horns blared as it merged onto Main Street in front of oncoming traffic.

"Goddammit!" Heading back to his truck, Bennett considered the implications of what had just happened. If they were watching him, it wasn't random. Whoever was after Mia knew about her life, about her past. He needed to see her, to warn her.

It would be another exercise in self-inflicted torment. Being in her presence was just too damned hard. Of course, the other option, of not passing the information on and then having something happen to her—yeah, that wasn't really an option. Climbing into his truck, Bennett headed west, toward Fire Creek and the distillery.

Mia emerged from the distillery, keys in hand. She was exhausted. Between the caregiver interviews, the full day's work she'd put in, and being torn up inside by the temptation of Bennett Hayes she felt completely drained. But she reminded herself, the last interview had panned out. She'd hired the former nurse who would start the following day.

As she approached her rental car, she felt the first stirring of awareness. With one sweeping glance of the parking lot, she easily identified the source of her disquiet. He stood on the other side of the street, leaning against his truck. Arms folded over his broad chest, the leather of his jacket stretched taut over heavily muscled arms and his long legs crossed at the ankle, that one look at him was enough to make her heart pound and the blood race in her veins.

There were other concerns though. He wouldn't be there without a reason. For him to come to the distillery, to risk running into her father, there was a damn good reason. Opening her car door, she tossed her laptop bag and coat inside before locking it back up and crossing the street to him.

"We need to talk," he said.

There was nothing that couldn't be said right there, but that wouldn't get her what she really wanted. A few precious, stolen moments wouldn't hurt anyone, she reasoned.

"So take me somewhere that we can," she replied.

He opened the passenger door for her. She climbed in

without hesitation and he closed the door behind her. In climbing into that truck, going with him without question, Mia knew that the battle that had waged within her had been decided. Whatever came, whatever chance she had, it would *always* be him.

They drove west, heading out of town. It was a familiar route, one they had taken dozens of times when she'd been a teenager. Sneaking out of her house in the middle of the night, meeting him at the road and riding off into the night in the old Buick that his father had given him had been the greatest thrill of her life. Every time, she'd been breathless and giddy. She'd forgotten what it felt like to be that happy, to have that sense of anticipation.

They drove for several miles, neither of them saying a word, even as he hit the turn signal and turned off the highway. The road to the abandoned spring house was rutted from neglect and had become, over the years, more mud than gravel. The truck slowed as they rounded the bend and finally stopped altogether.

By rights, the building should have been falling in on itself. Looking at it, she saw that pieces of wood had been replaced here and there, the roof patched. Someone, and she had a sneaking suspicion who, had maintained it carefully. It was a bittersweet thought. "I missed this place," she said softly.

"I come here when I need to think," he said. There was a defensiveness in his tone that told her it was much more than that.

"We all need a place for that," she replied. "Why did you come, Bennett?"

"I needed to talk to you. I can't call you. Can't go to your house. Ambushing you at work is the only thing I could think of," he said simply.

Mia glanced at him out of the corner of her eye. Her gaze was drawn to his large hands, draped casually on the steering wheel. They were callused and scarred and she wanted to feel them on her skin more than she wanted her next breath.

"Generally speaking, when people say that, it's bad," she replied. Her voice was thin, breathless.

Bennett turned toward her then, his face drawn, expression fierce. "I saw them—the driver of the SUV."

That effectively doused her insta-lust. "What? When did this happen? Where?"

"They were parked across the street from Revision today. When I spotted them, made a move toward them, they took off." He climbed out of the truck.

Mia waited as he walked around to open the door for her. It was a familiar ritual.

"Why did you approach them?" she demanded. "That could have been dangerous!"

"I was hoping to get a look at them. Confront them. They're not the only ones who are dangerous," he replied.

She left that alone. The cold fury in his tone was not something she'd ever heard from him. It didn't mesh with the boy she'd once known. While that boy was still very much a part of who he was, there were new layers to him that she didn't know, didn't quite understand. "Did you see them?"

"No. The windows were tinted well beyond legal and the tags were so covered in mud they were impossible to read. Oddly enough, the rest of the vehicle was spotless."

Mia walked toward the spring house, her steps slow and even a little timid. She was walking straight into her past, but she wasn't certain yet if it was wise. Regardless, it was inevitable. "Is it safe inside?"

"Safer than it was when we used to come here," he answered.

She smiled at that as she reached for the padlock on the door. "Is this your doing?"

She heard his footsteps behind her, felt the weight of his presence. His arm brushed against her as he reached past her and unlocked the door. A shiver moved through her.

"Yes," he admitted. Grudgingly, he added, "I don't like sharing this place with other people."

"Even me?" she asked.

"You're the reason I don't want to share it. Coming here..." He paused for a second, his gaze sweeping over the building, "it's like church. Sacred."

The little bit of hardness that had remained inside her, the shell she'd cultivated to protect that wounded part of her, shattered like glass. "I'm so sorry, Bennett."

"For what?"

She turned to him, her eyes filled with tears. "For hurting you. For not being brave enough to fight for what I wanted. For letting every day of the last ten years pass without reaching out for you."

Bennett sucked in a breath. Those words cut into him, slicing right to the bone. They hurt, but it was a release at the same time. For years, he'd wondered if she had regrets, if she ever questioned the fateful decision she'd made that night. There were other answers he needed from her, but for the moment, that was enough.

"And now? Are you willing to fight now?"

"I can't," she answered. "I have reasons for the choice I made, Bennett. Those reasons still stand."

His fists clenched at his sides. It was either that or punch the damn wall. "So why climb into my truck? Why come out here with me? I could have told you everything I needed to standing right there in front of the distillery."

She stepped through the door and into the darkened interior of the spring house. Her words floated back to him with a slight echo. "Because I'm selfish. I wanted to be alone with you, away from prying eyes, away from all the reminders of why this is a terrible idea. Because I wanted to give myself an opportunity to give in to temptation."

Bennett walked in behind her and closed the door. The spring still flowed through, the sound of the water moving over the rocks and boards was strangely peaceful. The mountain of obstacles separating them was still there, an elephant in the room that, for the moment at least, he would happily ignore. Instead, he focused on one part of her confession alone. "I tempt you?"

She glanced over her shoulder at him, her dark hair falling into her face. He reached out and tucked it behind her ear. It was a gesture he'd made hundreds of times, muscle memory. But it was Mia, and nothing was ever simple. Even that relatively innocent touch was like a match to tinder.

He reached for her, pulling her close. She didn't fight, didn't resist, she just melted into him. The softness of her body settled against the hardness of his own.

Bennett closed his eyes and let the heat and spark of that sink into him. Her arms wrapped around him and he buried his hands in the thick fall of her hair. A gentle tug and she tipped her head back until their eyes met.

"I can't promise you tomorrow, Bennett."

"I didn't ask you to," he said, his voice tinged with desire and anger. She frustrated him. She infuriated him. And for better or worse, she had put her mark on him a long time ago.

Mia's gaze was focused on his face. The light coming through the windows was harsh, casting him half in shadow. Every plane and angle of his chiseled face was highlighted. Bennett wasn't handsome. He was beautiful.

"Damn you, Mia," he said, his voice rough and deep. "You've been a fire in my blood for half my life."

Those words burrowed into her, sneaking into the place deep inside her where the last bit of hope and innocence was sheltered. She wanted him as much as she ever had.

"What are you going to do about it?" she challenged.

The fist buried in her hair tightened, bordering on roughness. She craved that from him. Her body pressed against his and she could feel the hardness of him. This wasn't the boy she'd once known. There were pieces of him still, but this man was rough, dangerous and there was an edge to him that made her yearn for something she couldn't quite name.

"Enjoy the burn," he whispered.

There was no chance to answer. His lips descended on hers. The kiss they'd shared in his kitchen had been gentle, tender. This wasn't. It burned just as he'd promised. His mouth moved over hers roughly, commandingly. He didn't simply kiss her, he consumed her, and she reveled in it.

Hindered by her cast, Mia wanted nothing more than to strip his clothes away, to feel the wicked burn of his skin hot against hers. Instead, she explored with her uninjured hand, delving beneath his jacket and the cotton of his T-shirt until she encountered firm muscle and warm skin. Without conscious thought, her hand clenched, her nails digging into his flesh, marking him.

Bennett broke the kiss, his breathing ragged. "You drive me crazy."

"I've missed this," she said.

"Just this? Or me?"

"No, not just this," she admitted reluctantly. "Everything. Hot, drugging kisses. The way it feels when you wrap your arms around me. All the little things you always did to make me feel special—I haven't felt special in a very long time."

His arms tightened about her, squeezing gently, infusing his heat and strength into her. "You should. Every day you should."

"Make love to me, Bennett."

He sighed, his breath ruffling her hair and warming her skin. "I want that so badly," he admitted. "But not here. At least, not now. It's too cold. The ground is too hard."

"I don't care about any of that," she replied. "As long as I'm with you. We've waited long enough, don't you think?"

He laughed, but it was a pained sound. "A few more hours won't kill us. I'll come to your house tonight. Sneak into your room the way I used to."

She shivered at that promise. "It's been a long time. Think you can still climb a tree?"

"I know what's waiting for me at the top," he answered softly. "You're a hell of an incentive."

When he stepped back from her, the sense of loss was immediate. She missed the heat of him, the pressure of his body against hers. "I guess this means we head back to town."

He took her hand. "We'll come here again when it's not freezing cold. But for now, you should go home and rest, because I promise you won't sleep tonight. But first, we talk about what happened earlier."

"The SUV."

"Mia, this isn't some random event. This person knows you, knows your history—our history. Why else would they have been watching me, too?"

"I don't know," she said. "I can't fathom any of this."

"Is there anyone that would have reason to hurt you? Have you fought with someone? Is there a jealous ex out there—well, besides me?"

"No. There are no exes besides you, at all. I told you, Bennett—I haven't had time for that. But—" She stopped, clearly hesitant to finish the thought.

"But what?"

Mia let out a heavy sigh. "Erica. She's the only person that I've argued with lately."

"Who the hell is Erica and what did you fight about?"

Mia moved toward the door of the spring house and looked outside. It had begun to rain. Fog was coming in off the river and was hovering low to the ground, creating an eerie and haunting landscape. "She's my father's latest mistress, and my coworker. There was this idiotic proposal she had at work to take some of our older reserve barrels which are worth ten times what the newer stuff is and mix them so that we could have more product to sell and to satisfy the waiting list."

He frowned at that. "There's a waiting list for Fire

Creek now? Y'all have never overproduced, but you've never run out of stock either."

"With the bourbon theft last year," she said, "prices for most craft and small batch bourbon went up, ours included, and we sold more. But we didn't have the stock because of—Bennett, if I tell you this, you can't say a word to anybody. Promise me?"

He glared at her. "When have I ever not kept your secrets?"

"You're right. I'm sorry. I didn't inherit my share of Fire Creek. I bought it. So did Clayton and Quentin."

He frowned at her, clearly puzzled by the admission. "Why would you have to do that when it would eventually be yours anyway?"

"Because my dad was driving it into the ground. If we hadn't stepped in, we would have lost everything," she said and then paused to take a breath. She'd never admitted that to anyone outside of her immediate family. "We had to sink every penny we had into the company to keep it afloat thanks to his mismanagement. Overspending, borrowing to the hilt for decades—but none of us knew how bad it was until we nearly lost Fire Creek altogether. As it was, most of our back stock, except for these few barrels, had to be sold via private auction in order to avoid foreclosure because of a tax lien."

"How the hell did you keep that quiet?" he demanded. "People in this town know everything!"

"Clayton worked with an auction house in Japan. Bourbon is very big there, you know? They managed the sales for us and Clayton oversaw the transport and distribution of the barrels." And in that month, because he'd played everything way too close to the vest, Annalee had filed for divorce. It was another sin to lie at Samuel's doorstep, she thought bitterly.

"Where does Erica fit into this?"

"We argued about her proposal. The day of the accident, just before I left the office, we had it out," Mia admitted reluctantly. "I wasn't especially nice."

"You could have been the biggest bitch to ever walk the earth and it wouldn't give her an excuse to try to kill you! Do you honestly think what you argued about is enough of a motive?" he asked.

"No, but I think she feels threatened. She knows I don't want her at Fire Creek and she knows that if given half the chance, I'd march her off the property myself and see her banned for life," Mia offered. "So, the argument, no... long-standing animosity and my general objection to her having anything to do with my family's company when it's her meal ticket? Maybe."

Bennett nodded. "I'll see what I can find out about her. Last name?"

"McCoy."

"Of course it is. Nothing like a Hatfield or McCoy reference to bring it all into perspective," he said. "I'll see what I can find, but for now, I need to get you back to your car and you need to get home."

She didn't want that. She wanted to stay with him, but it was impossible. Stolen moments were all they'd ever had. "You'll come to the house tonight?"

He smiled at her, his expression laden with wicked promise. Then he stepped forward and took her hand. "There's not a power on Earth that could keep me away."

Mia smiled as he led her back outside to his truck. She had waited years. Waiting a little longer would only make it sweeter.

E velyn, the lady who sat with her mother during the night, had already arrived and helped get her ready for bed. By the time it was done, Patricia's bed changed, a fresh nightgown on her and everyone settled in for the night, Mia was burning with anticipation. Bennett would be there soon.

Mia showered quickly, careful to keep her cast covered. Somehow, she managed to shave her legs with only one hand. She returned to her room, wearing only her robe and her hair still piled up in a ponytail. It seemed a little too obvious to greet him wearing nothing, and lingerie, which would have been even more obvious, had never quite made it onto her shopping list. It was a pointless purchase for her as no one would ever see it.

Looking through the drawer, she finally settled on an ancient T-shirt that, if she thought back, had probably belonged to him at one point. She'd just managed to get the shirt on when she heard the soft knock at the window. Turning, she saw him there, perched on the ledge. Instantly, she was transported back in time. Their first kiss had been right there in her bedroom. She'd been terrified they'd get caught, terrified that her father would murder him for even looking twice at her, much less putting his hands on her.

Of course, it was different now. She knew what to expect, she knew just how he could make her feel, and the anticipation of that had left her breathless and eager already. Crossing the room, she unlatched the window and raised the sash.

"I thought you might not let me in," he said. "It looked like you were having second thoughts."

"Just memories," she replied. "The first time you ever kissed me was right here at this window."

He smiled at that, a sheepish expression crossing his face. "I was scared to death."

"Of what?"

"That you wouldn't let me, or that you would. That your dad would come in and my body would never be found," he admitted. "Even if he had, it would have been worth it."

"Well get in here before they find your body on the ground."

"So you doubt my tree climbing abilities?"

"No," she replied snappily. "I doubt the strength of those limbs. You've added a few pounds since you were eighteen."

"So now I'm fat?"

She rolled her eyes. "Stop fishing for compliments and just get in here."

He grinned, and shifting his legs over the windowsill, he slid into the room with the same grace he'd always possessed. Watching him playing sports in school, she'd always been struck by the easy way he moved. Everything he did seemed effortless and easy.

"Second thoughts?" he asked.

"No," she said. "I'm just wondering why the hell you're taking so long when I'm standing in front of you without any underwear on."

She didn't have to ask twice. Within seconds, he'd closed his arms around her and tugged her close. Through the thin cotton of her T-shirt, the heat of his body against hers was scorching. With the hard press of his body against hers, Mia let out a soft sigh of contentment. Then his mouth was on hers, his lips playing over hers with a wicked skill that left her breathless and yearning.

Memories came rushing back, only to be swept away beneath the onslaught of that kiss. This was no tentative boy. This was a man who knew how to kiss, who knew how to seduce. He robbed her of the ability to think. It left her breathless and weak, her knees trembling and her body buzzing from the fire he'd stirred in her.

Somehow, without her even realizing that he was doing it, he's moved them both backward across the room. When the backs of her knees bumped against the side of the bed, she opened her eyes in surprise. He pulled back from the kiss for just a moment and stared down at her, his expression hungry and fierce.

"If you're going to change your mind on me, Mia, do it now, while I still have the strength to let you."

She smiled up at him, lifted her hand to his cheek. He'd shaved but she could still feel the slight prickliness of his recently trimmed beard. It was so different from when they'd been younger, but she yearned to feel it against her skin. "I haven't changed my mind. I want you. I never stopped."

He kissed her again, slower, more tenderly, but the fire was still there. Then he laid back on the bed and took her in his arms. With her head resting on his chest, Mia closed her eyes in contentment. For a split second she wondered if it would have still been that way for them if she'd run away with him a decade ago. Would they still want one another so fiercely, or would that fire have burned out?

"You're thinking again," Bennett murmured accusingly.

She laughed softly. "A little. I just wondered if I had met you that night, if I'd gone away with you when we were so young and, honestly, so stupid. Do you think it would have worked? Or would we have just wound up making each other miserable and hating one another the way so many couples do?"

"I think we would have fought. I think we would have made up. I don't think that I could ever hate you. But you wouldn't be living in a house like this. You wouldn't have the things you do now," he said. "Or did, before you sank every penny into the family business."

"It's useless to wonder about a past that can't ever be reclaimed," Mia admitted softly. "I'd rather focus on the future right now—the immediate future."

Taking initiative in a way that surprised them both, Mia moved over him, her thighs parting to sit astride his lean hips. She could feel his hardness pressing against her through his jeans and it spiked her own need.

"That was a bold move," he said with a wicked grin.

She looked down at him and then reached for the hem of her shirt. Without any hesitation, she lifted it and slowly stripped it over her head. Naked, completely bared to him, she said, "I've been celibate for a decade, Bennett. I'm out of patience."

His gaze roamed over her, potent, weighted like a touch. She felt it on her skin. Then his hands followed, slowly, reverently. He traced every curve, his callused fingertips creating a delicious friction on her skin.

"My god! Do you not know the meaning of hurry?" she asked.

"No." He shook his head. "No. I'm not rushing anything. I want to savor every minute."

Mia groaned in frustration, but as his hands moved to her breasts, his fingers teasing her already hardened nipples into taut peaks, it morphed into a cry of pleasure. Then he reared up and took one taut bud into his mouth, his lips closing gently over it.

"Don't make me wait," she pleaded.

Their eyes met. "You could tempt a saint," he said. "And I've never been accused of being that."

Mia arched against him, eager for more. "Please, Bennett!"

He retrieved a condom from his pocket and then reached between them to unzip his jeans. Mia shifted, rising onto her knees as he rolled the condom on. When he was done, she closed her hand around him, guided him to her entrance and then sank down slowly, taking him in.

The breath shuddered from her body as the sensation overwhelmed her. His hands settled on her hips, his fingers digging into her flesh, holding onto her as he surged upward. Mia's head fell back, her back arched as his name fell from her lips on a broken sob.

It was a slow, easy rhythm to start, but like everything else between them, it soon raged out of control. Their movements became faster, more urgent. The tension built inside her, every muscle growing taut. Just as she would have cried out his name, he grasped her hair and tugged her down to him, kissing her hard. He rolled her to her back and then surged into her again.

Mia felt the first fluttering contraction of her orgasm, then another. She clung to him as the waves of pleasure washed through her, and then she felt him stiffen, his body growing taut before he shuddered against her. He whispered her name, a soft and breathless sound against her ear as they held onto one another.

Utterly spent, Mia snuggled against his chest and refused to think about the future or the past. Instead, she vowed to hold on to that perfect moment as long as she could.

Mia was late getting to the office the next morning. Rushing in, she ran smack into her brother in the hallway. Quentin caught her before she went tumbling in her ridiculously high heels.

"Where the hell are you headed to in such a hurry?"

"I overslept this morning," she lied.

The last thing she wanted was to get into a conversation with Quentin when she was feeling guilty for rolling around in the sheets all night with Bennett. Quentin would lose his mind and that was just more drama than she wanted to deal with on less than a couple of hours of sleep.

"Are you feeling okay? You look tired."

Great. Just freaking great. "Don't ever tell a woman she looks tired, Quentin. Those are fighting words. It's no damn wonder you're single," she snapped.

Quentin shook his head. "You're in a mood. Damn. Clayton's no better. He's mad as hell about something, but damned if I can get it out of him."

Mia grimaced. Clayton was normally the most even tempered of all of them, but when he was in one of his moods, he could be the devil. "I'll talk to him."

Quentin rolled his eyes. "Great. I'll take cover now before you all start taking potshots at one another."

"We can be professionals, which is more than I can say for you. Didn't I see you wearing that suit yesterday? Where did you spend the night?"

Quentin blushed, but stood his ground. "I don't answer to you, little girl."

"You don't answer to anybody. That's part of the problem."

One of his dark brows lifted in derision. "Mia, I'm not poking around in your love life, much as I might like to offer an opinion. You need to back off that topic."

Effectively shut up, Mia nodded. "Fine. You mind your business, and I'll mind mine. I'm going to go see Clayton and see what's going on with him."

"Right. 'Cause even though I don't want you in my business, I am a-ok with you poking your nose in his."

Mia patted his shoulder as she walked past him toward the stairs that would lead to the offices that perched high above the warehouse floor. "You didn't come to dinner last Sunday. Are you coming this time?"

Quentin cocked his head. "Do you think she knows? Do you think she has any idea whether we're there or not?"

It was a question she had no answer to. Doctors and specialists had told them so many different things over the years that there was simply no way to know. "I hope so. I like to think that she does. But regardless of that, I know. I know I am there for her whether she understands it or not."

He looked at her for a moment and there was something dark behind his eyes. It wasn't anger. It was pain. Quentin struggled with their mother's condition more than any of them, but he rarely ever spoke of it. "I'll see you Sunday," he finally added. "I'm heading to Knoxville for the next two days. I'm meeting with another distribution company down there to see if we can't expand the market a little once our next batches are ready."

"It's going to be a lean year," Mia warned. "Once the waiting list is fulfilled, we're not going to have that much left for distribution."

"Rule number one, little sister," he said, walking away. "Leave them wanting more. We'll wet their whistles for our bourbon down South. Maybe we'll start a new waiting list."

Mia watched him walk away, a spring in his step. Clayton was good with the hands on, day-to-day running of the distillery. He loved the process of making bourbon, of staying in touch with the family's history that way. Quentin loved the wheeling and dealing aspect of working with distributors and sales channels.

For her, she liked holding on to the family's history, but she didn't make any mistake about her place in the business. There were other people who could take her place and do what she did. It didn't require any special skill, though she supposed the tourists coming in off the Bourbon Trail did like to be guided through the distillery by someone who was actually a Darcy.

Heading up the stairs to Clayton's office, she knocked softly and waited. He barked out a command for her to enter, and Mia's eyes widened slightly at his tone.

"I take it you're having a bad morning?" she asked, walking into the office.

Clayton's hair was mussed, his jacket was off, sleeves rolled back and his tie askew. It was just after nine in the morning and he looked ready to throw in the towel. "You might say that. Dad has been shopping again."

"Shopping for what?" she asked, taking a seat across from his desk.

"Women. Erica is in an uproar, threatening to quit. The problem with that is she knows all about this company. She knows about the massive auction of our product in Japan."

"So she has the power to sink us, and now she has the motivation to do so," Mia surmised.

"That's about it. So, don't piss her off any more than necessary, okay? I can't put out any more fires today."

"What other fires have you had to put out?" she asked.

Clayton looked up then, but his face was shuttered, his expression completely unreadable. "Nothing important," he said, shutting down further questions. "I've got work to do and so do you. If you want to look into working with Keenland, I need that proposal by the end of the day and Mia, make damn sure that Bennett Hayes climbs down that tree outside your window before daylight next time, okay?"

She blinked at him. "Excuse me?"

"Annalee brought the munchkin to me this morning so I could take her to school because she's going to Louisville for something."

"What's she going to Louisville for?"

Clayton's mouth firmed. "I'm not her husband anymore. I don't get to ask those kinds of questions. Point being, she saw him shimmying down that damn oak tree. Do what you want, but for the love of God, be discreet."

"Were you or were you not the one who told me to go for it?"

"Yes. Go for it. Enjoy it. You deserve this and a hell of a lot more, but be smart about it. Samuel gets wind of this and everything I—" He stopped abruptly.

"Everything what? Clayton, just tell me what you're doing. You've been keeping secrets and I know they're about him and it's costing you everything. Tell me and I will help you."

"I can't," he said. "The things I'm working on, Mia, they're not really above board. I'm not cutting corners with the business. I would *never* do that. But to get what I need on him, to get the upper hand that I have to have to make this work, I can't play by the rules. And I won't let anyone else take those risks."

"What things are you working on? Clayton, for the love of all that's holy just tell me! You're keeping all those secrets and it's going to be the death of you."

He shoved his hands in his hair. "As much of a shit as Samuel's been to us, fucking people over isn't restricted to family. I'm digging, Mia, digging up every bit of dirt and filth on him I can. You can't do that without getting a little dirty yourself."

"What have you done?" she asked, her voice a fearful whisper.

"Nothing that I can back away from. Not yet, anyway," he answered softly.

"This isn't good for you," she said, her eyes brimming with unshed tears. Clayton was the best of all of them. He had a better heart and was just generally a more decent human being. It was eating away at him.

"No, but he isn't good for anyone. And if I can build a life here, for all of us, that he doesn't get to taint with his presence, it's worth the cost. So just be smart. Be discreet. And let me handle Samuel when the time comes."

Mia didn't say anything else. At that point, she figured a dignified retreat was her best option. Heading for her office and the mountain of paperwork waiting there for her, she decided keeping her head down and staying out of her brother's line of sight, and Erica's, was her best option for the remainder of the day.

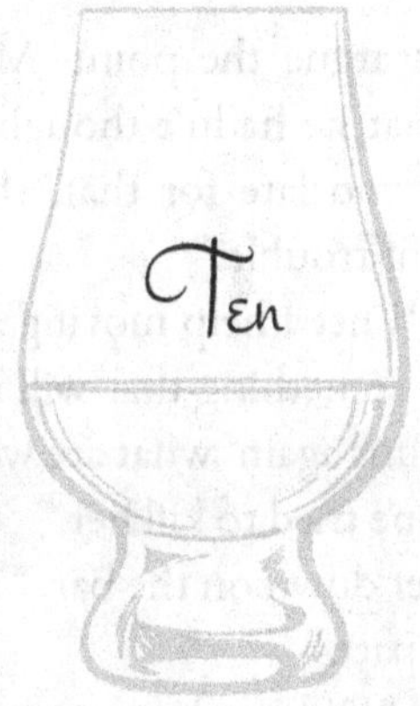

Ten

Bennett walked into the bar on Mill Street in downtown Lexington wearing a decades old T-shirt that he'd stolen back from Mia that morning. He'd told her she could have it back when she stripped it off of him. He was still grinning about her short and very blunt response to that while scanning the sea of faces. It was lunchtime and the crowd was thick, but he could see Matt Crawford's shaved head standing a good six inches over everyone else's.

"Bennett," Matt called out unnecessarily. "Over here."

Bennett sidled up to the bar and ordered a beer. At just twelve thirty, it was a little early, but it had been a hell of a night. "Hey, man! Thanks for meeting me."

"No problem," Matt said, clapping him on the back. "You piqued my curiosity. What the hell is going on in Fontaine these days?"

Bennett looked around casually. "I need a favor, it's about Mia."

"That can of worms needs to be closed, sealed,

burned, and the ashes fucking scattered. Will you never learn?" Matt said.

Bennett didn't argue the point. Matt wasn't saying anything to him that he hadn't thought himself a dozen times over. "Little too late for that, the thing is, Matt, she's in some kind of trouble."

"On a scale of 'I need help moving a couch' or 'could be going to jail for something that will never allow me to vote or own handguns again' what are we talking about?"

"I think someone tried to kill her."

Matt set his beer down on the bar. "You're gonna have to back up on that part."

Bennett sighed. "Did you hear about the accident?"

"Yeah. Wet roads and a spin out. She drives like a bat out of hell. Always did."

"I know that," Bennett said. He explained about the car, the tracks at the scene, and Mia's reports of a dark SUV. "Then I saw it. Parked across the street from Revision."

Matt shook his head. "That's all circumstantial, Bennett. Yes, it's fishy, but it doesn't mean anything."

"I approached the SUV and they took off so fast they left half their tires behind. There's something to this, Matt."

Matt leveled a hard stare at him. "I'm not saying you're wrong. But you could be reaching. You like to be the hero. More to the point, you like to be *her* hero."

"That's not what this is about," Bennett said, his tone even and without heat.

On a heavy sigh, Matt asked, "So who am I checking out?"

Bennett smiled. "It's nothing major. Her name is Erica McCoy. She works at Fire Creek and she's dating, if you want to call it that, Samuel Darcy."

Matt rolled his head on his shoulders. "Thanks for bringing this shit to my door. No one ever just calls me to go out for a beer."

"We're still having a beer," Bennett said. "I'll even buy."

"In that case, I'm getting a better brand," Matt said and signaled the bartender. After he'd ordered another round, he turned back to Bennett. "You know my sister was tangled up with a Darcy a while back. They have any relatives in Ireland as far as you know?"

Bennett laughed. "Don't give me shit about this when you're doing fishing of your own."

Matt didn't even bother to look guilty. "Loralei had it bad for this guy and he really did a number on her. I don't have anything against Mia, Clayton, or Quentin, but they're not a bunch you want to tangle with if you don't have to."

"Why is that?"

"Because they're all still circling around Samuel like he's the center of the damn universe," Matt answered. "Milk curdles when that son of a bitch walks past it. Never did like him."

"Tell me how you really feel," Bennett said with a grin before taking a long pull from his beer.

At that point, Matt's phone went off. He cursed. "Looks like you're going to have to owe me that beer for a while longer. I'll text you anything I find out about Erica McCoy, specifically any vehicles registered to her that might fit the description."

Bennett thanked him and watched Matt go. While he was in town, he thought he'd swing by and see Loralei. Heading out of the bar, he walked the few short blocks to Loralei's shop. Set between an upscale wine market and a jewelry store, it screamed "money."

Opening the door, the little bell above it tinkled. Immediately, Loralei came from the backroom, holding some creature in his hand that might, if you stretched the imagination to the breaking point, be considered a dog. "What the hell is that thing?"

She wagged her finger at him. "Haven't seen you in a month of Sundays and the first thing you do is insult my dog?"

Bennett grinned and then hugged her, ignoring the disgruntled huff from the creature in her hand. "Baby, I hate to break it to you, but whoever told you that thing was a dog—well, they just lied."

"This is Churchill," she said, pointing to the tiny, black pug that was snuggled in her hand.

Against his own better judgment, Bennett gave the little thing a scratch on its head. Immediately, its tongue dropped out of its mouth and it was panting happily. "All right. It's a dog. I wouldn't call it a smart dog, but it's a dog."

"Oh, no. Churchill isn't smart," she agreed readily. "He's a dumb as a box of rocks. It's part of his charm. And speaking of charm, what brings you to town? You never come here!"

He lifted the pug from her hand and cuddled it. It couldn't be more than a few months old. "Why on earth did you slap a dignified name like Churchill on this poor ignoble creature?"

"He isn't named after a prime minister," she stated, moving behind the counter. "He's named after the cigars that belonged to my stepfather. After he chewed up the last one, Franklin told Mama that he had to go."

Bennett winced. "That had to be ugly."

"Oh, it was. Franklin was shouting down the roof, but that's the benefit of being somewhat less than brilliant like

Churchill here. People yell and scream and you just don't care," Loralei added, with a cheeky grin.

That smile took him back to days of cutting school and cruising around in an old beat-up car with her and Mia and whatever boy Loralei was crushing on at the time. She'd never settled on any one of them for long, though. Still, he missed those days. Sunshine and giggling girls in short shorts. "I've missed you. You ever coming back to Fontaine?"

"As long as my mother remains married to Franklin Bell, that would be a big no. She comes to town, we have lunch. She tells me I'm fat and should only order a salad. I cry. She gets offended and goes home. It's our monthly routine," Loralei added. "What about you? You can come to Lexington anytime you want. I keep telling Savannah whenever I see her that she needs to think about opening up another store here."

"It's on the table," Bennett said. "We need to build up our stock a little more, but the damn stuff sells quicker than we can make it or find it. Speaking of siblings, I just had a beer with your brother."

Loralei rolled her eyes. "What was he bitching about now?"

"He's not real fond of your ex-boyfriend. Wondered if maybe there was a family connection between your ex and mine."

"Matt needs to learn how to keep his mouth shut," she said quietly. "I don't know if Ciaran has any connection to the Darcys or not. We're not exactly on speaking terms these days."

"Did you ever wonder?"

She shrugged. "He was very good at distracting me whenever I asked questions about his past. Now, I've got a question for you, Bennett! Why are you suddenly so interested in the Darcys again?"

Bennett considered telling her, but then thought better of it. Loralei would be nothing but a cheerleader for him and Mia, but there was no point in getting her hopes up just to dash them. Mia had made it very clear that whatever was happening between them at the moment was only temporary.

"Just curious," he hedged.

"I have never, in all my life, seen two people who belonged together more than the two of you."

"She left me, remember?" There was a little bit of anger in his voice, a little bit of the hurt pride still rolling under the surface.

Loralei looked at him archly. "She had reasons. Good ones that you don't understand yet. Hopefully, someday you will."

He shook his head. "You still stick together on everything, don't you?"

"I might not see her often anymore, but I'll always have her back. And vice versa. Don't break my girl's heart, or I'll make you pay." Loralei picked up a necklace from the display stand he'd been staring at, a confection of sheer ivory ribbons and amber beads. She put it in a gift box and handed it to him. "Give that to her when you see her. I thought of her the minute it came in."

He didn't deny it. There was no point in even trying. Instead, he kissed Loralei's cheek, then headed for the door. "I'll be seeing you," he said softly before exiting her shop and heading home.

Mia left the office a little early. She'd completed the paperwork she'd had to and anything that wasn't completely necessary, she'd put off 'til the following day. Preoccupied with thoughts of Bennett, she hadn't been able to concentrate through most of the day.

The eagerness she felt for him, to be near him, to have his touch, was terrifying. But, she reflected, at least she was feeling something again. The unending, numbing sameness of her days had finally broken. There was something that she looked forward to, something that she feared losing. It had only been days but all the old feelings had come back almost immediately. But then she could admit, they'd never really gone away. Her relationship with Bennett had never ended, it had just paused.

Climbing behind the wheel of her rental car, she made the relatively short drive home without incident. She wasn't paranoid, but she did find herself checking the rearview mirror more frequently, watching the road a little more carefully.

Entering the house through the back door, she hadn't noticed her father's car parked out front. Walking into the kitchen, finding him seated at the island, drinking iced tea and smiling flirtatiously at her mother's new caregiver was not how she'd envisioned ending her day.

As always, Samuel was the epitome of an elegant and distinguished southern gentleman. His suit was perfectly tailored. His silver hair was well groomed and combed back from his high and perfectly bronzed forehead. He could easily have graced the cover of any magazine that catered to the old money set. It was a look that he'd always admired and strived to emulate but there was a darkness underneath it all. He was selfish to the bone and ugly with it to the depths of his soul. As far as Samuel Darcy was concerned, everyone was fair game as collateral damage as long as he got what he wanted in the end.

"What are you doing here?" she demanded, uncaring that her tone was clearly cold and unwelcoming.

The caregiver, Elizabeth, gave her a sharp glance, but said nothing, as Samuel turned toward her with a cool glare.

His smile was perfect, all gleaming teeth and dead eyes like the shark he was. "That's hardly an appropriate greeting for your father, is it?"

"Excuse me," Elizabeth said and left the room quickly, obviously unnerved by the acrimonious undercurrent.

"You're hardly an appropriate father, are you?" Mia shot back with a bitter laugh. They had an arrangement that worked. They saw one another at the office when he deigned to show up otherwise, he stayed far away from her mother and from her.

He set his glass down on the countertop, his controlled movements a stark contrast to the fury in his gaze. "I am your father, regardless of what you think of me. You won't take that tone with me, girl."

"I'm not a girl. I'm a grown woman. And you don't live here anymore. You hang your hat wherever your latest twenty-something mistress lives. You don't get to just walk in and make yourself at home."

"But I do," he said with a smirk. "My name is still on the deed. The woman in that bed, in what used to be my office, is still my legal responsibility. By law, as her husband, it is my duty to see to it that she is appropriately cared for."

Mia sneered in disgust. He made her skin crawl more and more every day. The very idea that his blood coursed through her veins made her feel tainted. "You've never once given a damn about what kind of husband you were to her, or what kind of father you were to us. You're a megalomaniacal, sociopathic bastard and we both know it. So just cut the crap. I don't have the time, and with your advancing years and bad habits, you definitely don't."

He continued as if she hadn't even spoken, probably because she was deviating from the script he'd already mapped out in his head. People weren't real to him, they weren't three-dimensional beings with thoughts and feelings of their own. Everything, in his self-absorbed and narrow little world, revolved around him. "Then, of course, there is my moral obligation to ensure that her caregivers have only her best interests at heart. You and I had an agreement, Amelia Renae, and I think you need to be reminded of that."

It shouldn't be possible to hate someone this much, she thought. The darkness, the bitterness and the consuming fury all whirling inside her should have swallowed her whole. Or if there was any justice in the universe, they should have incinerated him on the spot.

"I'm unlikely to forget it. And if I should," she added, "You're always eager to remind me."

His gaze was hard and cold when it settled on her. "The way I see it, your overnight guest violated the terms of our agreement. You were supposed to stay away from Bennett Hayes."

"Spying on me?" she asked, opening the refrigerator and grabbing a bottle of wine. She poured one for herself but made no motion to offer him any. When he reached for the bottle, she snatched it back and placed it in the fridge. It was a small gesture, but she felt small inside. Mean and petty and full of fury.

"You're not making it difficult, what with him climbing out of your bedroom window in the wee hours of the morning," he said. "But you always did like to court gossip."

"And you liked to court everything else, though court might be too rarified a term for some of the women you've entertained." He had her on the defensive and she didn't like it.

He rose to his full height and stood close to her. It was an old tactic, intended to intimidate her. Somehow, over the years, it had lost some of its power. "Mia, we've not seen eye to eye in a long time, but you are my child and I naturally want what is best for you. That will never be Bennett Hayes."

"I didn't assume it would be," she replied coolly.

"Then why are you making this so hard? You know what you have to do, Mia," he said, and his tone was deceptively soft and contrite. "You have to end it."

She hated him more for pretending to care than for not caring at all. He could couch his protests in any manner he liked, but the truth was, he didn't like Bennett because of his last name. There'd never been any reasons beyond that. He deemed the Hayes family too low on the social scale and too close to old scandals that could tarnish the Darcy name. It wasn't about what was good for her. It never had been.

Taking a deep shuddering breath, she met his gaze and refused to back down. She was violating the spirit of their agreement but not the letter of it. It was a tactic she'd learned from him. "Right now, I can't take care of Mama physically. Until my wrist heals, I have to depend on others to do that for me. Once it's better, everything goes back to the way it was. And as for our agreement, I never said I'd stay away from Bennett. I said I wouldn't run away with him, and I didn't. So you have no reason to be here."

Samuel nodded thoughtfully. "It really would be a shame for the truth to come out, for people to realize the hand that Hayes—and you—played in your mother's unfortunate accident. People might not look so favorably upon him and his sister in their little enterprise if it were discovered that your mother's life, in all but the basest of essences, was taken from her as a result of the selfishness of the two of you."

It didn't matter how many times he reminded her, the twisting of that particular knife would never cease to hurt. But then Samuel was always good for going for the jugular.

"Yes, and you're always so eager to point it out," she replied. "Whatever is happening between Bennett and myself, it is temporary. He knows that, and so do I. There's no need for you to concern yourself, but there is every need for you to get the hell out. The sight of you sickens me."

He leaned closer, his face only inches from hers. "You forget who has the power here."

"I've forgotten nothing. Not the way you cheated on her before she was even injured. Not the way you manipulated, controlled, and lied to every one of us. I haven't forgotten that you nearly bankrupted the family business. I. Haven't. Forgotten. *Anything*." She finished with the last words coming out between clenched teeth. "I'm done with this conversation. You can see yourself out."

"I've warned you, Mia. You're my daughter and I don't want to hurt you, but I will break him. Whatever it takes."

"Why do you hate him so much? What the hell did he ever do to you?"

"He reminds people that we might not be entitled to everything we have, and I can't let that happen," Samuel replied. "Do him a favor and cut him loose. But if you—in your all too familiar, selfish and stubborn ways—have to have your fun, do it. Then you can break his heart all over again."

He left, the door slamming behind him, and Mia actually felt the temperature of the room go up. Her blood was boiling and her stomach churned in the aftermath of their bloodless conflict.

The caregiver came in then, carrying the empty bottles used in her mother's tube feeding. "I'm sorry about all that," she said. "I didn't realize that you and your daddy weren't on the best of terms or I wouldn't have invited him in."

"He has a key," Mia said sharply. Realizing that she was being a snappish bitch, she forced a smile and softened her tone before continuing. "It's fine, Elizabeth. He can be very charming and very persuasive. He also likes blondes. I'd be wary of being too charmed by him, if I were you."

The woman nodded her understanding. "I will certainly keep that in mind."

Wanting desperately to change the subject, Mia asked, "How is Mama tonight?"

"She's doing fine," Elizabeth said, clearly just as eager to escape the awkwardness. "I gave her a bath earlier and did her hair. Nothing fancy, just a braid. I thought it would be more comfortable for her in bed like that."

Mia smiled sadly. "That was very thoughtful of you. Do you need help turning her or getting her repositioned?"

Elizabeth shook her head. "Not at all. She's all settled in. I'll turn her again in a couple of hours. She's been fed for the night...it isn't my place to say, but I think she's in there. I think your mama hears and understands everything going on around her. I worked as a nurse for five years, mostly on a unit taking care of people in similar conditions. You can tell when they know."

Mia felt the tears burning behind her eyes. The words had been said kindly, and she appreciated them in that light, but at the same time, it scored straight to the bone. The idea that her mother was there, aware and just trapped inside her own body was a double-edged sword. It meant, on the one hand, that there was hope. On the other, it meant that Patricia Darcy was in a daily, living hell.

Mia drained the remainder of wine in her glass, and as an afterthought, grabbed the rest of the bottle from the fridge. Looking like a lush, under the circumstances, was the least of her concerns. "Thank you for that, Elizabeth. Since you don't need me, and I'm not feeling the best, I'm going to head upstairs for now. I'll check in on Mama later."

Elizabeth sighed. "I'm sorry. I shouldn't have said what I did. I spoke out of turn—."

"Not at all. I'm glad that you see her, that she's a real, whole person to you. Excuse me. It's been a long and difficult day."

Mia climbed the stairs feeling like she was a hundred years old. In the safety of her room, away from any prying eyes, she stripped off her jacket and the high heels that she hated and laid down across her bed. Much like she had as a brokenhearted teenager, she hugged the ancient teddy bear she'd had since she was a child and just let the tears flow.

Downstairs, Patricia lay in her bed. Quiet as always. The television was on, the low hum of voices doing little to penetrate the quiet of the room. There was the monotonous beeping of her IV machine and the steady drip of fluid through the tubes. While her fluid needs could be met well enough with her tube feeding, the anti-convulsants required to keep her from seizing were another matter. In the deeper shadows of the room, someone moved. The lamp on the desk in the corner clicked on, followed by the ruffling of papers. Drawers opened and closed. The file cabinet was next. It was chocked full of old homework assignments and home-made cards. Tax returns from more than a decade ago were in there along with old bank statements.

"What are you doing?"

The intruder gasped, then jumped, bumping

painfully into the corner of the desk. "Don't sneak up on me like that, Beth!"

"Elizabeth," she corrected. "As of now, Mia has no idea who I am. She barely remembers anyone from high school unless it's Loralei Crawford or Bennett Hayes. Speaking of which, I expect him to be sneaking in here anytime for another tryst so if you're going to search, you better do it quickly and quietly. I heard you from the kitchen!"

"Don't take that tone with me!"

"Mother, I took this position, working for a woman I can't stand, just so you could find whatever it is that you're looking for. But we don't have forever."

"This is for all of us, Elizabeth! If this comes out, then your father is ruined—all of our chances are ruined!"

Elizabeth eyed her mother coldly. "I can see why you and Samuel were drawn to each other. You're just alike. Though I can't imagine two people as cold-hearted as the both of you ever managing a truly torrid affair. The night caregiver will be here at nine. That means you need to be gone by eight thirty."

Twelve

Bennett took the path through the woods to Mia's house. They hadn't agreed to meet that night, but then again, they hadn't agreed not to. She might welcome him with open arms or she might have gotten cold feet and push him right out the window.

"At least I won't be bored," he muttered aloud. As he neared the backyard, he paused. Patricia's caregivers were on a routine schedule, but that didn't mean someone hadn't stepped out back for a breath of fresh air or a secret smoke. When he didn't see anyone immediately, he moved past the back porch and hooked his foot on the first branch of the oak tree.

Sneaking around with Mia, meeting with her under the cover of night, it would be fun for a while. But he knew there would come a point when he wanted more. What would suck more than anything was that there wouldn't be a doubt in his mind that she wanted it too. That didn't mean she'd reach out and grab hold though.

Mia was stubborn to the core and whatever it was that made her so convinced they couldn't have anything more than a few stolen moments was something she wouldn't share with him until she was damned good and ready. He had to admit that there was every possibility she never would.

By the time he reached her window, he was slightly winded. Looking in, the lights were still on and he could see her curled up on the bed, her clothes askew and her hair a mess. An empty wine bottle was on the night-stand. She looked like hell, like she'd done battle with the day and the day had won. But she still took his breath away, he stopped for a moment just to take in the sight of her.

The window was cracked, so he didn't knock, just lifted it slowly and let himself in. He didn't approach her immediately, but took a seat on the impossibly tiny bench in front of her dressing table. Hell, that's what he thought they were called, anyway. All he knew for sure was that it was covered with makeup and bottles of God only knew what all that undoubtedly cost the earth.

On the bed, Mia stirred, rolling onto her back. Her eyes opened slowly and a slight frown turned her lips downward in a pout that was far more appealing than it ought to have been.

"You're being a creeper," she said.

"If I were truly a creeper," he replied, "I wouldn't have just been watching you sleep."

"Fair enough. I didn't think you'd come here tonight."

He considered his answer carefully. Pushing her would only make their situation more difficult, but there was some nasty, bitter part of him that wanted that. The fight, the big blow up was coming. If they burned off a little steam now, they might avoid it for a while longer. "I wasn't sure that I would either. But we both know this—

whatever the hell is happening between us—it has an expiration date."

"So that means you just let yourself into my bedroom whenever you feel like it?" she demanded.

"No, that means if you want me I'm here, and if you don't, just say the word. You're not the only one who can walk away."

"Is that supposed to bring me to heel? You threaten to walk away or throw the past back in my face and I'm supposed to just roll over and offer myself in apology?"

They were both mad, and he was smart enough to know that it had very little to do with what they'd said and much more to do with all the things that had been left unsaid between them for so long. "Goddammit, Mia! I'm not here to take potshots at you!"

"That's not how it feels from over here," she snapped back as she sat up in the bed and attempted to right her clothes.

Bennett knew of only one effective way to shut them both up and keep either of them from saying something that there was no coming back from. He stalked toward the bed, reaching her in two long strides. Without thinking, he gripped her upper arms and hauled her up until she was pressed against him. He took her mouth, claiming it, kissing her with all the anger, all the pent-up fury and hurt from a decade of wondering just where the hell things went wrong.

She kissed him back with the same intensity, with the same mix of anger and pain, but riding just below all of it, was the undeniable need for each other. It coursed between them like a fire out of control. Her nails scored his back through his clothes, even as he was tugging at her blouse, buttons popping and skittering over the floor.

With her blouse torn open, he brought his hands up

to cup her breasts. The hard points of her nipples against his palms only fueled the blaze. When she bit his lower lip, her teeth tugging at it less than gently, only to be followed by the delicate sweep of her tongue, he was lost.

More roughly than he should have, Bennet pushed her back on the bed. Moving on top of her, he shoved her skirt up and gripped her panties, tugging them down over her hips until they tangled at her ankles.

It wasn't just that he wanted her, it was that he needed her to crave him. Maybe it was pride, or maybe it was just his own overblown ego, but he wanted her begging, and he wanted her to know that no one would ever make her feel the way he did.

He felt her shiver beneath his hands as he gripped her thighs. He kissed her, his lips and tongue moving over skin so soft that it defied reason. Then he nipped with his teeth and felt her shiver beneath him. Her hand found its way to his hair, threading through the strands. But she didn't push him away. She tugged him even closer.

He inhaled deeply, drawing her scent into him. Then he parted the slick folds of her sex and settled his mouth over her. She tensed beneath him, her hips arching up as a shuddering cry escaped her lips.

Bennett didn't offer any reprieve. He tormented her relentlessly, his tongue moving over her heated skin, circling the hardened bud of her clit without ever quite making contact.

Again and again, he offered more only to withhold the relief at the last second. She was burning under him, her body trembling and her breath coming in sharp pants. He slid one finger inside her, teasing her, offering just enough to keep her wanting more.

Her hand in his hair tightened again, tugging forcefully. "Bennett, so help me God, if you don't stop torturing me this way…" she hissed out between clenched teeth, unable to finish the threat.

He didn't smile, but it was exactly the outcome he'd wanted. Deliberately, slowly, he moved his mouth closer until his lips were poised above the most sensitive part of her. Drawing it gently between his lips, he sucked at her clit with long, slow pulls, savoring the taste of her and the sharp, shattered cry that escaped her. Flicking his tongue over her, he felt the first pulse of her orgasm, but he didn't take that as a cue to stop. He wasn't done with her, not by a long shot.

Mia shivered, her whole body convulsing with the unparalleled pleasure he was giving her. Bennett had always been good. Even when they were young and had more enthusiasm than skill, he'd always made sure she was taken care of. But this was beyond that. This was him proving a point and proving it well.

He was relentless, driving her to that brink over and over again. Finally, he'd given her what she needed and let her coast over that edge. But that didn't mean he was done with her. Every movement of his lips, of his skilled and wicked mouth was designed to wring every last bit of pleasure from her.

He drove her over the brink again, one orgasm rolled into the next until her whole body trembled with it. Sweat slicked her skin and she was breathless.

"Bennett, please…no more," she finally pleaded. It was too much, too intense. She felt vulnerable and exposed, as if he'd activated every nerve in her body.

He rose above her, unzipping his jeans, "This might

be temporary—I might be temporary for you, but by god, Mia, you will never forget me or that we'll never burn for anybody else the way we do for each other."

Mia couldn't think, couldn't even attempt to respond to that. Her whole world had concentrated to the point of contact between them, to the sensation of his hard flesh sinking into her, branding her.

His hands gripped her forearms, raising her hands above her head and pinning her to the mattress. He was making a point of her vulnerability, of his strength, but even then, he wasn't hurting her. The part of her mind that was still even remotely functional, acknowledged that he never would, he never had. She'd been the one to cause pain in their relationship for both of them.

Tears formed, and she didn't have the strength or even the awareness to blink them away. She was caught up in a maelstrom of sensation and emotion. The unrelenting physical pleasure and the driving need for more swirled with the regret and the abiding pain of knowing that whatever they had was finite.

Thinking of that, of the coming moment when she wouldn't have him anymore, Mia let go of thought altogether. She focused entirely on the present, on the feeling of his hands on her, of him moving inside her. The tension built again, coiling tight, and when it burst, he was with her, her name falling from his lips like a curse.

In the aftermath, her body still shaking and neither of them able to move, they were both quiet. When he finally rolled off her, they both stared up at the ceiling for the longest time, until the stony silence stretched taut and uneasy between them.

Finally, unable to stand it any longer, she rolled to her side and looked at him. "I'm sorry."

"What the hell are you sorry for? I'm the one acting like a fucking Neanderthal."

"For pushing you away. For pulling you close. For repeating the cycle a dozen different times before this is all done. I'm selfish enough to want you, and selfish enough to have you even when I know it isn't good for either one of us," she admitted.

He looked at her and his expression was hard, unreadable. "It isn't just you. I'm a grown ass man, Mia. I know we're going to hurt each other. I could walk away right now if I wanted. But I'd rather have a little piece of you than nothing at all."

"You're braver than I am. Half the time, I just want to cut and run now, before it hurts too much."

He sighed. "I don't understand why...I've never understood. Is it just because my last name is Hayes? Yes, your dad fucking hates me, but what man isn't hated by the father of the woman he's sleeping with?"

"Bennett, I—that's part of it. He never let me date. I wasn't sneaking around with you because of your last name. I was sneaking around with you because that was the only way I ever got to date anyone! But yes, you being a Hayes makes it more complicated."

"Mia, if you'd tell me, I could help you—whatever it is."

"You don't want to know, Bennett. Trust me!"

His expression changed, his eyes narrowing. "Mia, did he ever hurt you?"

She laughed. "This isn't a *Lifetime* movie. Unless you count manipulation and verbal abuse, no. He never laid a hand on me."

"That's enough," he responded, though his relief was evident.

"You can't fix this. You can't take it to your shop and

reshape the pieces to make them all fit. We have this. We have right now. And when my hand is better, and the money for round-the-clock care for Mom runs out, then we go back to the way we were." She took a deep breath. "Unless you want out now. If you do, I understand. I'm moody. Bitchy. Sometimes mean and hateful. There's nothing here for you that's worth the trouble."

He closed his arms around her and pulled her tight, her face pressed against his chest. "You're wrong. Not about the first part. You are all of those things and then some. But you'll always be worth the trouble."

Mia felt the tears threatening again. Rather than give into them, she focused on something else altogether. "You're not keeping this shirt. It's mine."

"It was mine first," Bennett replied evenly, though she could hear the smile in his voice.

"I had it for longer," she protested.

"We can fight about this all night, or..."

"Or what?" she asked.

"You could persuade me."

Mia sat up and looked at him, taking in the wicked gleam in his eyes and the grin on his face. This, she thought, was the flirting, laughing boy she remembered. "And how exactly am I supposed to do that?"

"I have a few ideas, but you're still wearing too many clothes for most of them." He paused. "For all of them, really. Honestly, naked is kind of the starting point."

Thirteen

Bennett was working on another one of Savannah's crazy ideas in the smaller and much more cluttered workroom at the back of Revision. Take this old and utterly worthless piece of barn wood, wire it for electric and add Edison bulbs, she'd said. He'd thought it would be the ugliest damn thing in creation, but now that it was done in the weird zigzag pattern she'd mapped out, it was kind of growing on him. He'd swallow his own tongue before he'd ever admit that to her.

The heavy, reclaimed barn door slid open with a scrape as it moved along the track. Savannah walked in, Matt Crawford on her heels. Matt wore a frown and stared at the overly exaggerated movement of Savannah's sashaying backside more intently than Bennett was comfortable with. Savannah had her own life, he knew that. But for his own peace of mind, he stayed as blissfully ignorant of it as possible.

"It's our very own little boy blue," she said, being her usual smart-ass self.

Matt glowered at her. "Your mother should have spanked you more often."

She looked back at him, her blonde hair falling over her shoulder in a way that was clearly, and deliberately, provocative and had Matt stepping back like he'd been sucker punched. Bennett wanted to choke her.

"I prefer to get my spankings from other sources these days. You're welcome to apply for the position," she said.

"I'm your brother," Bennett said. "And I'm right here. In this room. Needing a massive amount of mind bleach. Fucking hell."

Savannah just rolled her eyes and left, calling out, "Don't faint. You're not wearing enough petticoats to cushion your fall!"

Matt was still shaking his head like a fighter who'd took one too many punches. When he finally looked up, he stared straight at Bennett in horror. "When did that happen? When the fuck did that happen?"

"What?" Bennett asked, moving the now finished piece to one of the other worktables. Savannah would come in and determine what to price it at and his mind would boggle at the fact that an hour's worth of work and a bunch of junk could fetch four figures.

"That! That succubus who just walked out of here is not your baby sister."

"She is my younger sister. I don't know that Savannah was ever a baby," Bennett replied.

"But pigtails, freckles and Hello Kitty backpacks do not turn into *that!*"

Bennett turned back to him with a raised eyebrow. "I'm starting to be a little concerned about how much you paid attention to her then. Even more by how much attention you're paying to her now."

Matt raised his hands. "Look, you know and I know,

that I would never violate the code. Sisters and exes are always off limits. But, *damn*, you could have warned me!"

Folding his arms over his chest, a better option than assaulting a police officer even if said police officer was an old friend, Bennett asked, "Is there some reason for this visit or did you just show up to make me uncomfortably aware of the fact that my friends routinely check out my little sister?"

"Fine. You're right. I am here for a reason. I didn't find anything on Erica McCoy."

Bennett nodded, but he knew there was more to it than that. "You would have called if that was all you found."

Matt pulled his phone from his pocket and rolled his thumb across the screen before handing it to him. Bennett looked at the picture of Erica standing arm in arm with another pretty blonde, similar in age. It was the Derby apparently, or possibly the Oaks, judging by the size of the hats they wore. It was the background that caught his eye though. They were leaning against a large, black SUV and in the corner was what appeared to be the edge of a deer guard.

"Who is she?"

"I don't know. Yet. All I could get from the post was a first name. I'm cross referencing it with vehicle registrations that match the one in the picture, but there's more holes in this than a sieve."

Bennett rocked back on his heels, considering the options. "Lay it on me. What exactly are we looking at?"

Matt shrugged. "The car may not be hers. The car in the pic may not even be connected. Erica may not be connected and, there may not even really be anything to be connected to. Still, I trust Mia. I trust you. And my gut says there is something up with all this. Too many loose ends that all point in the same general direction."

Bennett looked at the picture again. "She looks familiar, but damned if I can figure out from where."

Matt nodded. "I thought the same thing. She is Samuel Darcy's type. Maybe he's cheating on his mistresses now."

"How in the hell any man could think having more than one complicated, demanding woman in his life at a time is a good idea is a goddamn mystery," Bennett said.

Matt pointed at him. "She's tied your dick in a knot again."

"Hell, she never untied it the first time," Bennet admitted gruffly.

Matt went back to the picture. "Pretty blondes are a weakness for two of the Darcy men in particular, but then there's Clayton. The odd one out. Divorced, divorcing maybe? I can't keep up with the relationship status of everyone in Fontaine. But I do know that no one seems to know why they split up."

"Irreconcilable differences."

Matt glanced at him. "Reading the gossip columns?"

"Having dinner with my mother," Bennett corrected. "Every Sunday like clockwork."

"Does she still make that pot roast? And the homemade mashed potatoes?" Matt asked.

"Yes. But if you come to dinner, Savannah will be there."

"Never mind. You know, maybe we're going at this wrong," Matt said.

"Dinner?" Bennet asked, then realized immediately that Matt had switched topics on him. "Dude, not all of us have ADD. You need a better lead-in."

Matt rolled his eyes. "Maybe Mia isn't really the

target. Maybe someone sees her as the instrument of revenge."

"That's a little Machiavellian, isn't it?" Bennett scoffed.

"Look at you with the big words! Happens all the time. And Samuel Darcy has pissed a lot of people off. He plays the game. Politicians love him, high society eats up his act, but we all know what a bastard he is."

"So what's next then? Assuming that Mia isn't the prime target, just the expedient one."

"You really did get a word of the day calendar, didn't you?" Matt said and then laughed at his own joke. Growing serious again, he continued, "I'll see if I can't get a last name. And I'll see if I can't scour the social media accounts and gossip columns related to the Darcy men and figure out which one is connected to our mystery woman."

"My money's on Samuel," Bennett added. "Quentin doesn't like to shit where he eats and Clayton is all business, but I could be wrong."

"You're not exactly objective about this topic," Matt pointed out.

Bennett nodded. "I hate that fucker. I'd never do anything to make it happen, but I swear to God, I'll laugh all the way to the cemetery just to piss on his grave."

"That's still illegal. Not as illegal as say, terroristic threats—unless there are kids present. But that's a whole different kind of crime and involves major address restrictions for the rest of your life."

Bennett chuckled in spite of himself. "You are an asshole."

"Yep. I hear that a lot. The thing of it is, he's been keeping Mia a prisoner in that house, taking care of her mother for the last ten years. If he'd do that to his own daughter, what the hell do you think he'd do to someone else's? There are more people with reasons to hate him than not."

"That's the damn truth."

Matt headed for the door. "I'm going to work this angle for a bit. See who Samuel Darcy has pissed off and if there's any connection to this woman, once I get an ID."

"Send that pic to my phone. I'll show it to Mia and see if it rings any bells."

"Be careful with all this. People do fucked up shit when they're desperate."

There was something in Matt's tone that alerted Bennett to the fact that he hadn't just come to talk shit or even share info. He'd been running away from whatever the hell he'd seen that day. "I don't ever want your job. How the hell do you think about this shit and sleep at night?"

"Bourbon helps," Matt offered. "You can buy me a bottle and we'll call it even. One big enough to fucking swim in, but make it the good shit, since you've got an in at Fire Creek and all."

"Keep me posted, will you? I don't like not having a bead on this."

Matt offered a salute. "I'm sneaking out the back. Your sister might demand my virtue as payment if I go through the front."

Bennett laughed at that. "We build a lot of shit here, but time machines aren't one of 'em."

After Matt left, Bennett continued cleaning up the workshop. There were other projects that needed his attention, but they were too big to finish in the time he had left for the day. Which meant that Savannah would just have him moving furniture. Heading out into the showroom, he saw Carter leaning over the counter flirting with a pretty young woman who was clearly more inter-ested in him than in the vintage jewelry in the case.

"Don't let him troll for dates in here," he said to Savannah.

"Why not? If the men who came in here weren't married or gay, I would," she replied. "Speaking of which, Matt Crawford is super-hot. How did I not notice that all those years ago?"

"I'm not your ride or die. We don't have these conver-sations," he said shortly.

"We could," she offered sweetly. "I'll paint your nails and you can share all the details with me about how Mia Darcy makes your heart skip a beat. Then I can tell you all about Officer McHottie and what I want him to do with his handcuffs."

"I'm leaving, and I'm telling Mom you need an exorcism."

"Do that and I'll tell you exactly which sections were highlighted in her copy of *Fifty Shades*. Mom goes to church because she has lots of things to repent...*lots.*"

"Leaving. Not listening," he called back and headed for the door, followed by the sound of Savannah's laughter.

Outside, the day was still cool, and the wind was howling. Crossing Main Street and headed for his truck, Bennett couldn't shake the feeling of being watched. Scanning the street, he saw nothing untoward. Fontaine was a small town, a short drive from Lexington and a farming hub. The vehicles lining the street ranged from the high end of luxury to loaded down with manure. There wasn't a black SUV with a deer guard among them.

Climbing behind the wheel of his truck. He picked up his phone and pretended to scroll through it, surrepti-tiously scanning the other cars. At the end of the street, a silver Mercedes pulled out. It was too far away for him to see the driver, but they didn't approach him, and instead headed out of town toward Lexington.

"Fuck. I'm paranoid," he said aloud.

With his phone already in hand, he searched the number for Fire Creek and dialed it, asking to be connected to Mia Darcy's office.

"This is Mia. Can I help you?"

Hearing her voice, all polished and businesslike, he smiled. "I certainly hope so."

"Are you crazy? You can't call me here!" she hissed.

"I need to talk to you. Actually talk. Vertically. Which doesn't happen unless we're in public. Meet me in Lexington tonight."

She sighed. When she finally spoke, there was hesitation in her voice. "Where?"

"There's a bar on Woodland. Mostly college kids."

"Loralei's go-to spot?"

"That would be it," he answered. "I'll see you there at eight."

Ending the call, he headed home to shower and tried not to be bothered by her reluctance. He wasn't cut out for being anyone's dirty little secret and it was sure as hell starting to get to him.

Fourteen

Mia pulled up in front of the bar. It was still early enough to manage a parking space in the lot itself, rather than on one of the streets nearby. After work, she'd gone home long enough to change clothes and make sure that Elizabeth had everything in hand for her mother.

Guilt gnawed at her. It seemed so wrong to be relieved to leave the house when her mother was stuck there, but it was a short reprieve, she reminded herself. Also, even though Bennett had said they were meeting to talk, it felt like a date, and she'd dressed accordingly. Now, the lacy camisole and skinny jeans with mile high heels seemed like poor form.

"Too late to reconsider," she muttered aloud. "You're already here, so suck it up."

Climbing out of the rental car and reminding herself that at some point she had to go out and shop for a new car for herself, something she dreaded worse than dental work, she headed into the bar.

"ID?"

Mia dug through her tiny purse and produced her driver's license, which the doorman gave a cursory glance at. It would have been a little more flattering if he'd looked a little harder.

"Ten bucks," he said.

Mia dug out a bill for the cover and then presented her right hand for the wristband.

"Need your left," he practically grunted.

She held up her cast. "Then you're going to need another one of those. One won't fit."

He grunted again and fastened the day-glow green band around her right wrist and waved her inside. Bennett was easy enough to spot once she was inside. He was seated at the bar, a beer in hand, and every female eye was trained on him. There might have only been ten women in the club early as it was, but every one of them had her eyes on him.

Letting her eyes travel over his long, denim-clad legs, the dress shirt that either Savannah or his mother must have bought for him, because he would never have chosen one that fit so well, and further up to his face, she stopped in her tracks. Every woman was watching him, but he was watching her.

The warmth of that soaked into her and she was greedy for it. After a moment, when it was obvious to every woman present just who he had been waiting for, only then did she step forward.

As she approached him, Bennett's smile shifted into a knowing smirk. "You do like to make an entrance," he said.

It wasn't an accusation she could deny. Instead, she just proved his point by leaning in, pressing her body against his and letting her lips hover just above his for a moment. Every eye in the bar was on them.

"And you like to be salivated over by coeds who were chugging screw top wine in their dorm rooms before they got to the bar," she shot back, but there was no heat in it, just easy humor. Her life might be a mess, her future was a bleak and depressing void, but there was one thing she was utterly certain of. He wanted her, no matter what.

"Is that why you came? Just to bust my balls?"

Mia kissed him then, just a quick, hard press of her lips to his. It was enough. She straightened, but kept her hand on his chest. It was a heady thing to touch him, to know that she could. "I have other plans for your balls, but they can wait," she answered and signaled the bartender for a drink.

"Well, that's a thought that's not going to leave me alone anytime soon," he replied and took a long pull from his beer.

Mia watched him from the corner of her eye, the play of muscles beneath the rolled back cuff of his shirt sleeve, the way his lips cradled the lip of the bottle. She was jealous of the damn beer.

"So, I could be at home, braless and in yoga pants, but I'm here instead. Why?"

"For the pleasure of my company," he replied. "And also because I talked to Matt today."

The bartender walked over. Mia ordered a whiskey and ginger. In a college bar, quality spirits were in short supply. Whiskey was a fine thing to mix with other substances, but polluting bourbon was just wrong. Once the drink was in front of her, she sipped it and frowned. "What did he have to say?"

Bennett placed his phone on the counter in front of her, the picture of Erica and her yet unknown friend on the screen. "Do you know her?"

"I *think* I do, but I can't—did we go to school with her?"

"If we did, she would have been ahead of us. She's pushing thirty in that pic and it's from a few years back."

"Erica is thirty-three. She's a little long in the tooth for Samuel, and according to Clayton, he's already shopping for a replacement."

Bennett nodded. "Sounds about right. This woman, whoever she is, has to be connected to Fontaine in some way. Matt, you, and I have all said she looks familiar, but none of us can remember why."

"Maybe it's not Fontaine that's the connection. You remember what it was like in high school. We'd meet up with the kids from Sayre or Lexington Catholic. All those parties on the river?"

"I remember those parties very well. That was the first time I ever got up the nerve to talk to you," he replied.

She smiled, thinking about how utterly beautiful he'd been with a sweet, shy smile on his too pretty face. "It took you long enough. I'd been putting myself in your path for three damned weeks."

"So, Matt mentioned something today that I think bears considering."

"I'm not going to like it, am I?" she asked, and took another sip of her slightly watered down drink.

"What if you're not the target, but the instrument?"

"I don't follow," she replied with a frown.

"Your daddy inspires a lot of feelings in people. Hatred. Envy. Admiration for those who don't know him well. And fear. He enjoys the abuse of power."

"Tell me something I don't know."

"All of this...hiding in a vehicle, watching, stalking. I think whoever did this is probably a woman scorned," he stated.

She considered it, and then nodded. It made sense. "I'd go along with that."

"It could be someone your dad blew off. It could also be Quentin. Or Clayton."

"Not Clayton," she replied instantly. "He's focused on other things right now and even if he wasn't, the only woman on his mind is the one who left him."

"Imagine that. Your brother and I do have something in common."

Her only response to that was a baleful stare.

"Right," he said. "Moving on. So Quentin and your father is where we need to look?"

"I'll just ask Quentin," she said. "He'll be at the house on Sunday for dinner."

"What are you going to ask him, 'Oh, by the way, dated and dumped any psychotic, murdering bitches lately?'"

"Can't hurt." Glancing around at the bar, she realized that ten-dollar cover or not, it wasn't worth being there. "Let's get out of here."

"And go where?"

"I've never seen Loralei's shop," she said. "We always meet at the house because of Mama, or she'll come by the distillery sometimes and bring me lunch. I want to see what she's done for herself."

Bennett threw a bill on the bar to cover their tab. "Can you walk in those heels?"

"Yes. Or I can take them off and go barefoot. It's practically summer outside even though we're a week from Thanksgiving."

"You're not going barefoot. There's enough busted glass on those sidewalks to kill a man. And while I'm not opposed to carrying you, it is about six blocks from here."

"Fine. But I'm finishing my drink and you're driving," she said.

"I'd never stand between a woman and her whiskey," he responded.

Ten minutes later, they were parked on the street in front of Loralei's shop. Opening the door for Mia, he helped her out of the truck and wondered how the hell she wasn't breaking her neck in those damned high heels. Of course, they did amazing things for her legs, and for her ass, both of which were pretty damned amazing to start with.

"This is gorgeous," she said, eyeing the window display. "I knew it would be. She's always had an eye for this sort of thing. She's like Savannah that way."

It was an easy comparison to make and there was definitely a similar aesthetic, he thought, considering the shabby chic vibe that the shop exuded. Realizing that the words 'shabby chic' had sprung, unbidden, to his mind, Bennett hung his head.

"I have got to spend more time with Emmitt and get the hell away from Savannah for a while."

"What was that?" she asked.

"Just quietly saying goodbye to my man card."

She laughed. "I missed you. I missed this. I mean don't get me wrong—hot, mind blowing, earth shattering, my thighs tremble for a day afterward, sex is all fantastic and wonderful, but you always made me laugh, Bennett, and I don't seem to do a whole lot of that anymore."

Bennett didn't say anything for the longest time. He just looked at her and could see the deep unhappiness inside her. Mia left him for reasons she wouldn't share, but there was no doubt in his mind that it hadn't been what she wanted. Somewhere along the way, someone, and he had a good idea who it had been, had convinced her that she had no other choice.

"You used to laugh," he mused. "You used to sit in the front seat of that old Buick while I drove down winding roads like a bat out of hell. You'd throw your head back and laugh like you weren't ever going to stop."

"Some of the happiest moments of my life were spent in that car," she said, walking past him to look at the other display window.

"I forgot to give you something. It's in the truck."

She laughed again. "That's a likely story."

He laughed at that himself. "Seriously. It's from Loralei. She gave it to me when I was in town."

Mia turned to him, and while her expression was fairly neutral, he could see the panic in her eyes. "You told her about us?"

He raised his hands. "Do not give me that look. Tonight is not for picking fights. And, no. I did not. But hell, Mia, it shows on both of us. Do you think anybody can walk around feeling what you and I feel for each other inside them and not have it show?"

"And what is it exactly?" she asked. "What do we feel for each other, Bennett?"

He shook his head and turned to face the window. "I'm not doing that. I'm not pouring my heart out to you when we both know this isn't going to last. I know what I feel. I know it'll hurt when you're gone. That's all you're getting from me."

"You're right," she said. "We shouldn't be fighting. If we're smart, we wouldn't even be near one another, but I don't really want to be smart."

"Then what do you want?" he asked, half afraid to hear the answer.

"I want to be that girl again," she said softly. "The one who throws her head back and laughs like she doesn't have a care in the world. Even if it's just for a little while."

"I don't have a Buick anymore. Think my truck will do?" he offered.

"If you've got a sleeping bag to throw in the bed of it, I know this spot down by the river—there's even an old spring house there," she said cheekily.

"I can probably come up with something."

Across the street, the doors to a restaurant opened, the sound of music and laughter spilling out into the street. Mia glanced over at the same time he did. Bennett heard her gasp and felt his heart sink. Samuel Darcy was exiting the restaurant, a blonde on his arm who was probably a couple of years younger than Mia.

She tugged at his hand. "We have to go before he sees us!"

It shouldn't have hurt. He'd known it was coming, he just hadn't expected it to be so quick. "Get in the truck," he said softly.

Mia did as he suggested, moving quickly and silently on those killer heels as she could. He walked behind her, realizing that was where he'd always be. As she climbed into the passenger side, she kept her gaze averted from the street. Hiding. Hiding because she couldn't allow herself to be seen with him.

The truth of it was uglier than he'd thought it would be. Closing the door behind her, he walked around to the driver's side and climbed behind the wheel. The drive back to the bar and her waiting rental car was short and silent.

"I feel like I did something wrong," she finally said.

"We've both been doing something wrong. I just don't get to lie to myself about it anymore," he answered.

"Bennett, it's not—"

"This wasn't your dad doesn't approve of me, Mia. This was you hiding like you were ashamed to be seen with me."

"There's nothing shameful about being with you, but things are just so complicated with Samuel. He has the power, Bennett, I don't. Not yet," she admitted tearfully.

It hurt him to see her cry, to see her need something that he couldn't—wouldn't—give her. But every time she hid like that, every time she reminded him that he was just a momentary distraction from her self-enforced prison, it ate at him. He was giving too much of himself, too much of his pride, and whether it was wrong or not, he couldn't keep doing that.

He took a deep breath, and started speaking words that would alter everything. "I had this thought the other night, sneaking into your room, that I wasn't sure how long I could tolerate feeling like your dirty secret. I just figured it out."

"Bennett, don't! Not like this."

"I can't do this, Mia. I could, actually. But I don't think I'd like myself much at the end of it, and oddly enough, that's important to me."

She hit him. Her balled-up fist slammed into his shoulder. There wasn't enough force behind it to hurt, but it certainly startled him. "You're doing this just to get even with me! All this was just some elaborate plan so that you could finally be the one to walk away!" she accused.

He looked at her steadily and let the ridiculousness of that accusation settle around them. "That's not who I am. You know that. Right now, I still want you. But not a piece. Not a stolen part. Not what's left after all the appearances have been kept up. It's all or nothing for me, and you're not ready for that."

"I can't...you don't understand!" she cried.

"Then make me. What hold does he have on you, Mia? What is this power that he has over you when you are a grown woman?" he demanded. It surprised him how quickly the hurt could turn to anger, how quickly he wanted to lash out at her and make her feel the same thing he was.

"It doesn't matter," she said, wiping her tears away. "None of it matters."

"It *does*. And if you ever figure that out, you know where to find me. But I'm not just going to sit there waiting for you. I've lived without you long enough to know that I can do it forever if I have to."

"On to the next one then? We're interchangeable? You're as bad he is," she said, throwing out the most hateful thing she could in his direction.

"That isn't true. And it's a hell of an accusation to make."

"Don't expect an apology. I can't. Not right now," she said, and that was as close to an admission of guilt or wrongdoing from her as he'd get. Under other circumstances, it would have made him smile. At the moment, it just made him hurt for her, for them both. Her pride and her secrets would cost them both what they needed most.

"You asked me earlier to tell you what we felt for each other. I'd call it love, but that's just a shadow," he said softly, his voice quiet in the cab of the truck. Her breath caught and she looked at him with tears streaming down her face and he saw the vulnerability in her, the loneliness that she had the power to end. He continued, "It's consuming. Needy. Mean, sometimes. I don't have the words...but that's as close as I can get."

"Bennett—" She stopped. Either unable or unwilling to say whatever was poised there on the tip of her tongue. He would have shaken her if he thought it would have done any good, but that would just be something else for him to have to live with.

Climbing out of the truck, he walked around and opened the door. Opening the glove box, he pulled out the little gift-wrapped box from Loralei and pressed it into her hands. For what he imagined would be the last time, he held the door for her as she climbed down to the pavement. "I'll send word to you if Matt finds anything else."

Bennett waited until she was in her car, waited until he saw her driving down the street, her movements precise and sharp. She was hurt, but she wouldn't fall apart. That wasn't her thing.

"Fuck it all," he murmured and headed back into the bar. A gallon of whiskey ought to cut it.

Fifteen

By the time she reached home, Mia was shaking. Her whole body trembled with the effort it took just to draw breath. She had known it would hurt. The notion that it wouldn't had never even occurred to her. Somehow, in the decade since, she'd convinced herself that she was tougher, stronger. Feeling so irrevocably broken inside, like all the hard and brittle pieces of her had shattered, was so much worse.

Climbing out of the car, she closed the door softly. It was either that, take control and be precise in everything she did, or she'd slam it hard enough to shatter the glass. As she neared the porch steps, she kicked off the heels that she'd worn primarily because she'd thought he'd like the look of her in them and threw them with as much force as she could muster. They landed disappointingly close.

As she took the steps up to the house, something caught her eye. The lights were on upstairs but not at the front of her house. It wasn't her room. It was the room that had belonged to her parents before everything had gone to hell.

"Who the hell is up there?" she said aloud. In that moment, it didn't matter. She was mad enough, hurt enough, reckless enough not to care. Unlocking the door, she let herself in and climbed the stairs quickly, pausing just long enough to grab the gun from the chest of drawers at the landing halfway to the top. By the time she reached the second floor, the light was off and Elizabeth was coming out of the room.

"Oh!" she screamed. "You scared me!"

Mia lowered the pistol. "What are you doing in that room?"

Elizabeth smiled, but it didn't reach her eyes. "I was just looking at family photos. I thought taking a selection of them downstairs and talking to Patricia about them might be nice."

Mia cocked her head to the side. It didn't ring true. Anger and heartbreak aside, she wasn't an idiot. "What would you say about them?"

"I'd tell her about Quentin and Clayton, of course... and you. All about Fire Creek."

Mia nodded. "I've never talked to you about my brothers. How do you know their names? How do you know which is which?"

Elizabeth's smile faltered then. "I really don't appreciate the inquisition. I was only trying to help!"

The picture from Bennett's phone flashed in her mind. It wasn't Elizabeth, but there was a resemblance. "Who was the blonde in the picture with Erica McCoy? Derby hats, a black SUV with a deer guard on it in the background?"

"I don't know what you're talking about," Elizabeth said. "You've clearly had a difficult evening, and I'm sorry for that. But I can't work under these conditions again."

Mia raised the gun. "I have had a difficult evening, so

I'd advise you to start being a little more truthful in your answers. Who was driving the black SUV, Elizabeth?"

Elizabeth backed away, pressing herself against the wall. "You're just going to shoot me?"

"Shoot. Not kill. Not yet," Mia answered. She wasn't even sure she was bluffing. "Who was the goddamn blonde in the goddamn picture with Erica McCoy?"

Elizabeth lost it then, letting out a screech that could curl hair. "My god, she's been dead for six years and all anyone still wants to talk about is my fucking sister!"

"Give me her damn name!"

"Why?" Elizabeth said. "She's got nothing to do with this, other than the fact that my mother couldn't bear to part with that monstrous gas hog of a vehicle that she loved! Katherine liked to get all dressed up and cruise around in that thing like she was still the goddamn homecoming queen!"

It all clicked then. Katherine Shelby had gone to school in Lexington. She'd been the homecoming queen, the prom queen, the head cheerleader and pretty much the envy of every teenage girl in Fayette and the surrounding counties. Her younger sister, Beth then, had been a pudgy, pimply-faced girl stuck somewhere in preteen hell. At one point in time, their mother, Barbara, and Patricia had even been friends.

Mia sized her up, noting the weight loss, the nose job, the skin resurfacing. It was a safe bet that Barbara was the driving force behind most of it.

"What happened to Katherine?"

Elizabeth shrugged. "She got drunk on a boat, fell off, and drowned. You can only party for so long before it catches up to you."

"If she had nothing to do with this, why are you here? Why force me off the road?" Mia demanded.

Elizabeth smiled again, and it was clear the woman was half deranged. "My mother and father have parlayed the loss of their beloved daughter into quite the political career. There's even talk of Daddy running for governor. But scandals are ugly, especially when your only claim to fame is family values and tragedy. Nothing can mar that squeaky clean image."

Mia was getting frustrated, tired of dealing with her. "What scandal?"

"My mother's affair with your father. The one that caused your mother's accident."

The world went completely silent. Mia's vision blanked for just a moment. It was like diving underwater. "What?"

Elizabeth sneered. "There's proof here somewhere. My mother's tearful confession written in a letter to your mother on the day of the accident. At one point, the bitch apparently had a conscience."

"Why would you help with this?"

"Why would you let your daddy control your whole damn life? We're broken people, Mia. I never thought I'd have anything in common with you, but there it is. We're both living these miserable, hateful lives created for us by destructive, selfish, toxic fucking people."

Mia lowered the gun again. "Get out. Just get your shit and get out. And if you or your bitch of a mother even look sideways in my direction again, I *will* put a bullet in you."

Elizabeth nodded. "My mother told me I should make friends with you to get in here. First time in my life I wish I'd listened to her. Under other circumstances, Mia, I think we would have gotten along just fine."

Mia watched her walk past and then down the stairs, following at a safe distance. When the other woman had left the house, she didn't just lock the doors, but bolted them and put the chains on. It wasn't something she'd ever felt compelled to do. Not in Fontaine, not even after everything that had happened.

"Toxic fucking people," she whispered aloud. "Truer words had never been spoken."

Rather than go up to her room, Mia walked into the library and sat down beside her mother's hospital bed. With the gun still in her hand, and still too terrified to put it away, she prepared herself to sit there till morning. No one else was coming in that house uninvited unless they went back out of it with an extra hole in them. "Mama," she whispered. "This has been one hell of a night."

She dropped her head onto her mother's bed. "I wish you could talk to me. I wish, more than anything in this world, that you could just tell me what I need to do."

There was no answer. There would never be an answer. Mia let the truth of that wash through her. It hadn't been hope that had kept her from accepting her mother's condition. It had been guilt. But freed of the belief that she had somehow caused her mother's accident, Mia could admit that there was every possibility that the woman lying there in that bed was only a shell. Whatever had made her Patricia, it was either gone or locked away so deep that it might never be found again.

She felt alone. Not just lonely or sad. She felt, in that moment, like the entire world had simply passed her by. Her mother was trapped by a broken body and mind, and she was trapped by guilt and the selfishness of others.

"I hate him," she whispered. Mia wasn't sure if she was talking about her father or talking about Bennett.

Mia reached for the remote, flipped the TV on and prepared herself to keep watch. Teresa would arrive at six for the day shift, then she'd get to work. She had some papers to find.

Digging her phone out of the pocket of her painfully tight jeans, she dialed Clayton's number. He answered, sounding out of breath and more than a little angry.

"What?" he barked.

"I'm not coming to work tomorrow," she said.

"Why the hell are you calling me about this?" he asked.

"Don't fucking take that tone with me, Clayton. I've had a hell of a night and I'm sitting here with a gun in my hand."

He got quiet. "Mia, don't do anything stupid—"

"I'm more apt to be homicidal than suicidal, you jackass," she snapped at him.

He breathed a sigh of relief into the phone. "Why do you have the gun?" he asked, going back to being his normally reasonable self.

"Because I came home and thought someone had broken in. Turns out the new caregiver I hired for Mama was snooping through the house looking for old love letters."

"I'm not following."

There was another voice in the background. A decidedly feminine and all too familiar voice. "Who's there with you?"

"I'm not at home," he answered.

"Oh, you're at home. Just not your home, although, since you're still paying the mortgage on it, I guess that's up for debate!" It was irrational to be angry at him, and honestly, she wasn't. She was just angry and looking for a place to put some of it. "I'm having the worst fucking night of my life and you're screwing your soon-to-be-ex-wife?"

"That is not what's going on here," he protested. "Mia, you've got to calm down."

"No, I don't. I've been calm. I've been quiet. I've done what the dutiful daughter ought to and I've spent ten years making up for something I didn't even fucking do! I'm finding those letters, Clayton, and when I do, so help me God, I may kill him."

"Kill who, Mia? Baby, you're worrying me—"

"Samuel," she said. "I can't talk about this anymore. Not tonight. I won't do anything stupid or reckless. I won't shoot anyone unless they're trying to break in. I promise."

"I can be there in ten minutes," he said.

He would, she thought. Whatever he'd been doing with Annalee that she didn't really want to think about, he would walk away from that to come and take care of her. She'd been selfish enough for one night. She'd hurt enough people that she loved for one night by being prideful and cowardly. A few more hours on her own wouldn't kill her.

"No," she replied quietly. "I shouldn't have yelled at you. I'm just angry and hurt and jealous. If you're with Annalee, it's where you ought to be. Stay there. I'll be fine. Just don't expect me in the office tomorrow. I'm going to be tearing this house apart from top to bottom."

"I can help you."

"Yes, you can." Her voice rang with a certainty that felt good, vindicating. "Whatever it is you're working on, whatever you're trying to do to destroy him, keep going. Don't stop until you have it. When this is all done, I want him left with nothing. Promise me that."

"Whatever it takes," he vowed.

"Now, go seduce your wife. Or let her seduce you. We like that sometimes."

He groaned. "That is really not what's happening here and for the love of God, just don't go there with me. I can't take it. Quentin is bad enough."

She smiled. Even through everything else, there was nothing like making a sibling squirm to bring joy. "Good night, Clay. I love you."

"Love you too, Mia-mine," he said, defaulting to the pet name her mother had used for her so long ago.

"You bastard. I thought I was done crying for the night."

"Maybe you need to cry. You can't bottle it up forever."

"I can try," she protested lamely.

"It doesn't work. Take it from someone who knows. Call me. Anytime. I will come right there if you need me."

"I know you will. Good night," she said firmly.

After ending the call, she looked at her mother lying in the bed. Patricia was still quiet, her sightless eyes barely blinking. "I wanted to talk to you, Mama, and now, I kind of feel like I did. I'll never tell him, but somehow my idiot big brother has turned into you."

Sixteen

It was nearly four in the afternoon. Mia had been awake for somewhere in the neighborhood of thirty-three hours. She was wild-eyed. Her hair was disheveled and she was covered in dirt and grime from places in the house she would never have dreamed to look for anything more than dust and cobwebs.

Throughout the course of the day, people had come and gone from the house. Teresa had looked in on her here and there, but by and large, had given her a wide berth. Quentin had somehow managed to get back from Knoxville early and had stopped by at lunch, no doubt sent by Clayton to check on her. He'd taken one look at her, dropped the food, which still sat untouched on the table, and had backed away.

"Can I help?"

Mia looked up to see Annalee standing in the doorway. "You look rested."

"He did not spend the night. I did not sleep with him," Annalee said. "Stop poking at my love life and I won't poke at yours."

137

Mia considered the options. "Done."

"So what am I looking for?" Annalee asked.

"Letters. Handwritten to my mother or father from Barbara Shelby. They may or may not be signed."

"Got it. Am I going to be grossed out by them?"

Mia nodded. "Probably."

Annalee grabbed one of the totes still covered in dust that had clearly not been touched yet. "Not to be too much of a nanny here but, have you slept? Or showered?"

"No, and I'm hot. Sweating like a whore in church. There's a lot of things you shouldn't be poking at right now," Mia said pointedly.

"Fair enough," she replied and opened the tote.

They worked in silence for the longest time, each one sorting through years of memories. It would have been a tedious chore, sifting through the boxes and crates that held the scraps and ravages of a life that hadn't ended, but had stopped just the same, if it weren't so damn heartbreaking. Recipes that would never be used. Photos that would never be added to family albums and marked with the precise and almost calligraphic handwriting of the woman who just hadn't had time to get to it all.

Maybe it was the lack of sleep, maybe it was her overprotective older brother sending in the troops to keep tabs on her. Whatever it was, Mia was just suddenly overwhelmed with emotion.

"This is what's left of her. This, right here, all these plans and tasks. I don't want this to be me someday. I don't want to look up and realize that I let my whole life be an accumulation of things that I thought I would do or have someday."

Annalee stopped, the papers clutched tightly in her hand. "Mia, I don't know what happened here last night. Or what happened here the night you intended to run away with him...but I do know, that in spite of everything, these last two weeks I have seen you smile more, laugh more, and live more than I have in the nine years that I have known you."

It was like a knife twisting inside her. Mia closed her eyes and willed the pain away. It wasn't heartbreak. It wasn't rejection. It was regret, and nothing had ever cut so deeply.

Annalee reached into the box and pulled out a photo, holding it up for her to see. It was taken at some point when Mia had been in high school, but definitely at some point after Bennett had been part of her life. There was a smile on her face that had only ever been put there by him.

Annalee's voice was soft. "For the last week and half, you've been this girl. A little older and a little wiser—well, *maybe* a little wiser. But I've never known the girl in this picture. I've never seen your eyes sparkle like this—not until recently."

Mia shifted from her knees and sat down on the floor with her legs crossed. "Do you regret it?" she asked.

"Regret what?"

Mia gave her a baleful stare. "Do you regret breaking up with my brother?"

"I regret feeling like I had no other option," the other woman replied cagily.

"That's not really an answer. Do you miss Clayton? Do you think about him and about how things might have been, or could still be, different?" The clarification was precise and measured and intended to prompt a straight answer.

Annalee looked up. "I thought we weren't going to poke at this."

"Changed my mind."

She shrugged and answered. "Of course, I do. I love him. I will always love him, but somehow, it just stopped being what it was supposed to be for us. He got quiet and distant, and I felt like a shadow moving through his life. Whatever was in his head, whatever was consuming him —he wouldn't share that with me."

"Clay doesn't do a whole lot of sharing, Annalee. That's not who he is. He's the fixer. Hell, that's why you're here right now!"

Annalee put the box she'd been sorting down on the ground and dusted her hands on her designer jeans. It was a different look from the boho chick that Clayton had brought home that first Christmas after their world fell apart.

Looking at her, Mia realized just how much her sister-in-law had changed. The free flowing hair had been tamed and her tattoos were covered with a perfectly ladylike sweater from Nordstrom. Everything about the woman in front of her was sedate, restrained, refined. Annalee looked more like the one of them born to an old Kentucky family. Where was the hippy, the artist, the woman who wanted to go topless on the beach for her honeymoon?

When she spoke, Annalee answered softly, but there was steel in her voice, a hard edge that revealed just how much it hurt. "I know that, Mia. I've always known that about him, but how he related to the rest of the world was not how he was supposed to relate to me. I was his wife. I deserved to have a piece of him that was just mine."

"I'm sorry," Mia said. "I wish I could make it better."

"We all wish that for the people we love. Whatever happens for Clayton and me, you're my family. Got it?"

Mia nodded. "I got it. And I'm guessing that it's time

to pick up Emma Grace from, what is it today? Dance, Girl Scouts?"

"A field trip to the candy factory in Bardstown. What the hell happened to just going to school?"

Mia said nothing further, but watched as Annalee left the room. The only thing her family seemed to have in abundance anymore was misery. And work, she thought, glancing at the tornado like quality of the room around her.

Forcing herself to move, since it was either that or collapse from exhaustion, Mia opened another cardboard box that had been brought down from the attic; she hadn't thought about it, but that was probably a better starting point. Patricia had hoarded every scrap of paper, but she'd always stored them carefully in totes or plastic containers. The cardboard was an afterthought, probably by Samuel or by her brothers.

It was mostly old bills, paid, that should have been thrown out years ago. Near the bottom, she found a stack of medical bills. They were from the aftermath of Patricia's accident. It was a horrible thing to be excited by, but she finally felt like she was getting somewhere, at least in the right time frame.

Another box down, her back screaming from sitting on the floor for hours and her eyes burning from exhaustion and dust, Mia reached for another one and swore it would be the last, at least for a while. She was midway through it when she found her mother's purse. Somehow, with test results and hospital bills, the whole thing had just been tossed in the box.

Her heart was pounding and her palms were sweating as she unzipped it. The smell hit her instantly. The pressed powder and lipstick smell that still permeated the fabric lining brought back a hundred memories. Tissues, a petrified pack of gum, a wallet filled with receipts too old and yellowed to read, and at the bottom of the bag, wadded into a tight, angry ball, was the letter.

Mia unfolded it carefully, smoothing creases with hands that shook. The first lines were innocuous enough, but then the tone of the words on the page shifted. This was no tearful apology, no mea culpa. It was gloating and hateful, and hardly thinly veiled at that.

Barbara Shelby hadn't sent a letter of contrition but superiority. She was lording it over her, one woman to another, that the husband had strayed. *People grow apart. Sometimes, the act of being a mother interferes with the act of being a wife.* There were a half dozen insults in there directed at Patricia to explain Samuel's infidelity. Not a one of them included the truth. He was a selfish son of a bitch and Barbara considered him a trophy, tagged and bagged.

Above all else, Mia took one thing from that letter. The date on it was the same date of her mother's accident. Digging in the purse, produced an envelope, hand addressed, no return and no postmark. It had been delivered by hand. Elizabeth, in her psycho rambling, had told the truth.

"It wasn't my fault," she whispered aloud. She'd said those words before. A dozen times over the years in moments of resentment, in moments of desperation and loneliness when she just wanted to run away and never look back. But she'd never said them with conviction. They'd never rang with any kind of truth for her.

Folding the letter and envelope carefully, Mia stuffed them in the front pocket of her jeans and after a few false starts, managed to get to her feet. She hadn't eaten, hadn't slept, and the turmoil of the last twenty-four hours had taken their toll.

Taking each of the stairs with caution, Mia made her way down to the kitchen. She opened the refrigerator and retrieved a soda. She needed the sugar and the calories at that point.

"You need to sit down before you fall down."

Mia looked back at Evelyn who'd come in early. No one asked about Elizabeth. Teresa and Evelyn had just agreed to each do a twelve-hour shift.

"I'll be fine. I'm gonna rest now, and I'll put all this back together tomorrow," Mia answered.

Evelyn walked over to the fridge and pulled out a few things, placing them on the counter. "You're going to eat this sandwich, and then you're going to bed. I don't want to hear a word about it."

"I will. I promise," Mia replied. "Thank you. For taking care of Mama. And me."

"You don't thank me for that, child. That is not how this works. I don't know what devil is riding you right now, but it's the very devil," Evelyn admonished sharply.

"I can't really talk about it yet," Mia confessed. "But there are going to be some changes. Big changes."

"Your daddy?"

Mia's expression turned sour and bitter, her lips firming into a thin, hard line. "I will never call him that again."

"Whatever you intend to call him, you better figure it out quick. He just pulled up," Evelyn said. "You don't have it in you to fight him today. Just, for once in your life, let it lie, girl."

"Evelyn, you should go."

"No. That is not happening," the older woman said fiercely. "You could be knocked down by a feather right now and that man is a bulldozer if ever there was one."

"I'm tougher than I look," Mia argued.

"You'd have to be right now, or we'd have had to bury you by noon today."

"Evelyn," she said, and drew in a deep breath. "Go. Really. There are things that have to be said that—well, you're entitled to hear them—but there are other people who ought to hear them first. I'll be fine."

The other woman crossed her arms. "I will go for the time being. I need to run home and let my monstrous dogs out for a while and put some supper on the table for Mac. I'll be back here by seven when it's time to change and turn your mother again. And he'd better be gone."

"He will be," Mia promised. "Without a doubt."

Evelyn shook her head, still muttering under her breath as she grabbed her keys and purse to head out the back door. She offered Samuel Darcy an icy glare for good measure. "You hurt that baby, and I swear to God, I will make you regret it."

The screen door closed with a bang as Evelyn walked out to her beat-up car.

Seventeen

Samuel Darcy glared at the still trembling door and the back of the woman who'd stormed through it. "That woman needs to be fired," he said.

"That woman takes care of Mama like she's the most precious thing in this world. She can call you every name in the book, as far as I'm concerned and dance a damn jig while she does it," Mia shot back with enough heat in her voice that he actually looked at her.

Samuel, she'd realized, never really looked at anyone. He sized them up at first glance, then whenever he spoke to them after, he'd keep his eyes on his phone, his watch, his latest acquisition. People were just things to him, and once you saw through his charm, it didn't take long to figure that out.

"You're in a mood," he snapped. "And you look like a goddamn indigent. What the hell is wrong with you?"

"I had a little run in with an old friend of yours," Mia said softly. "Actually, it was her psycho bitch of a daughter, but let's not put too fine a point on it. Elizabeth was

145

here at Barbara's request. Evil is nothing without quality minions."

"You're babbling. I didn't come here for nonsense."

"Did you come to tell me another lie? To tell me that my adolescent selfishness destroyed my mother?" She laughed, but the hard, brittle sound would never be mistaken for humor. "Oh, you can't, that particular line is already used up."

He sighed and pinched the bridge of his nose, as if she were a constant trial to be borne. "Mia, I did not come here to fight with you or to tolerate this overly emotional drama you've wrought—"

"That I've wrought?" Mia gaped at him, astounded at his arrogance. "You did this to her!"

His jaw firmed and his mouth twisted into a thin, cruel line. "She drove that car, Mia. She's the one who slammed it into a tree because she was being reckless!"

"Because you broke her!" she screamed at him. "With your lies and your cheating and your manipulation, you pushed her to leave! You let her walk out of this house devastated and clearly not capable of driving. You weren't driving the car, but you sure as hell didn't try to stop her from doing it! And now, all of this, my whole life has been devoted to taking care of her. All the guilt, all the responsibility that I shouldered for years, and all along, *you did it!*"

"We will discuss this when you can behave rationally," he shouted, oblivious to the fact that he was just as irrational at the moment as she was. A vein throbbed in his forehead and his face had flushed with anger. "I'm not going to stand here and let my daughter yell at me! We are Darcys, Mia. Whether you like it or not, you are my blood, and we are above this!"

"You're not above anything," she replied flatly.

"You've lied, cheated, stolen, and broken every promise you've ever made. Listening to you talk about family honor is enough to turn my stomach! I'm done, Samuel. I'm just done."

Every part of her felt heavy, as if weighted with lead. She didn't know what to do. Even knowing that it had been a lie, reading that damned letter, saying it to him, confronting the thing that had held her prisoner for a decade left her more deflated than jubilant.

He grabbed her arm and hauled her back. "You don't walk away from me! You don't ever turn your back on me!"

She spun around and pushed back at him until he stumbled. "Or what?" she demanded.

He shoved her then, hard enough that she hit the wall and her head bounced off the plaster. Her vision flashed and dimmed before finally returning to normal. Somehow, she managed to stay upright

"If you want to leave, then leave," he sneered. "But this house, and everything in it belongs to me. If you walk out, you do it with nothing but the clothes on your back."

Mia considered her options. She had no car, no money. All that she'd managed to save from her salary had been eaten up paying for caregivers for her mother. Everything else was tied up in the distillery. Yes, she owned twenty percent of it, but what she and her brothers had been paying themselves was barely enough to get by. But the other option, remaining under his roof, was one she couldn't abide. "Then I'll go," she said simply. "Evelyn will be back at seven. I assume you can spare two hours of your life to care for the woman you destroyed."

"What I said all those years ago still stands," he threatened. "You'll never see your mother again. I'll put her in a home, and you won't be permitted to even cross the threshold."

"I'm not eighteen anymore. I'm older and a hell of a lot smarter," she replied. "You are her husband, and by law, her guardian, but any judge can overturn that and appoint someone else."

He said nothing, just stood there with his chest heaving like a bellows. The fury that rolled off him left her unmoved. It wasn't what she was doing, it wasn't guilt or defensiveness at being caught in the lies. It was just wounded, angry pride because she dared to defy him. "I will fight you tooth and nail," he finally said. "Just to prove you wrong."

She had never considered that he wouldn't. "Given your well-publicized affairs and recent scandals, not to mention the crazy ass Stepford daughter of your former mistress tried to murder me—I don't think I'll have a problem getting a judge to agree that you can't possibly have her best interests at heart. So you do what you feel like you have to, but be prepared, you son of a bitch, because I'll do the same."

He grabbed her hair and hauled her forward. Until that day, Samuel had never touched her in anger. He'd shouted, he'd ridiculed and manipulated, he'd guilted her into conforming to his will, but he'd never physically harmed her. As he dragged her toward the door, Mia fought. She kicked, clawed, elbowed and did everything in her power to make his life hell.

By the time they'd reached the door, they were both shaking and out of breath. His face had turned a shade of purple that, at any other time, would have caused her concern. In that moment, she hated him enough to wish that he would have a stroke or a heart attack. She'd put

him in the same kind of nursing home he'd always threatened to put her mother in.

"Get out," he gasped. "Get out and don't come back.
If you want to run with that white trash, do it, but you'll
never step foot in this house again."

Mia grasped the doorknob and twisted it. "I'm not
leaving because you made me. I'm leaving because I can't
bear the sight and stench of you any longer. This," she
said, "is *my* choice."

With that parting shot, she stepped outside into the
cold, frigid air. Panic hit her, twisting her stomach into
knots as she worried about who would take care of her
mother. Clayton. She needed to call him, but her phone,
her purse, her clothes, everything was inside the house.
She was standing on the front porch in her bare feet with
nowhere to go.

Go to him. That little voice whispering inside her
mind was more temptation than she could resist. Go to
him. The phrase came again to her mind—louder,
stronger and with a clarity that left no room for indeci-
sion. Broken down by everything that had transpired, she
needed him, if he'd have her.

That thought brought a fresh wave of panic for an altogether different reason. As Mia stepped off the porch, the
first raindrop fell, splashing on the bare skin of her arm. She
didn't fight it or bemoan the fact that one more thing had
gone wrong in her miserable life. Instead she embraced it.
She'd let the rain wash her clean and rid her of all the poison
in Samuel's lies and machinations. He'd made her his
puppet and for years, she'd done exactly what he wanted. It
was time, she thought, to do what she wanted and to do it
out in the open. No more secrets. No more hiding.

Her steps quickened and she ignored the cold as she

walked down the driveway toward the road that would lead her to Bennett Hayes.

Bennett sat on his couch, feet propped on the coffee table and a beer in hand. The UK game was on and he was doing his damnedest to be interested in it. The truth was, he was having a hard time being interested in anything. Things with Mia had ended on a note that he didn't much like.

It wasn't just that it was over. He'd been an ass. He knew it and he didn't like it. But there would be no chance to apologize, no chance to make things right. He'd laid down an ultimatum knowing full well that she wasn't ready to make those kinds of decisions. He'd pushed and she'd pushed back and now it was done.

He lifted the bottle to his lips again only to discover it was empty. "Fuck," he said as he rose to his feet to retrieve another beer.

"Bennett!"

At the sound of Carter calling to him from the porch, Bennett cursed again. "What the hell do you want?"

Carter had come over to watch the game, but he'd been acting weird as hell and had gone outside more than ten minutes ago with his cell phone. The whole thing was bizarre.

"Bennett, get your ass out here! Now!"

Bennett rubbed the back of his neck and tried to erase the tension that had gathered there, but it wasn't going anywhere. Reluctantly, he crossed the living room and stepped out onto the porch where Carter stood staring out into the rain. "What the fuck is it?"

"You've got company," Carter said simply and pointed.

Bennett looked in the direction Carter indicated. She was walking along the road, wearing the same shirt and jeans she'd had on the night before. They were soaked through. Her hair was plastered to her skin and even from a distance he could tell that her skin was all but blue with the cold. What the hell was Mia doing?

She turned at the end of his driveway and walked slowly toward them. At first he thought she was shaking from the cold, but he realized as she got closer that she was crying.

Bennett stepped out into the rain and approached her. "Are you crazy? It's freezing out here! Where is your coat?"

"It's at the house. Samuel wouldn't let me take it," she said between hiccupping sobs.

His jaw clenched. "What do you mean he wouldn't let you?" Over Mia's shoulder, he saw his aunt's door open. His mother, Carter's mother and father and a few cousins had all come outside to see what the hell was going on. *Of course. Of fucking course.*

She looked up at him, her eyes wet with tears and rain. If the swelling around her eyes was any indication, she'd been crying for a while.

"You wanted to know why I didn't come to meet you that night. Why I didn't run away and marry you when I was eighteen," she said.

He looked up at the audience across the way, they were clearly not going anywhere. "We don't have to do this now. Not out here in the cold."

She glanced at the people gathered on the porch. "No. People want to know. You wanted to know. It's time it all came out," she said with a sniff. "The day I was supposed to meet you, Samuel told me that my mother's accident was my fault. That on the night she crashed her car, she'd been out looking for me while I was sneaking around with you."

It felt like a punch to the gut. "Mia—"

She held up a hand to stop him from speaking. "I need to finish this, Bennett. Please. If you stop me, I don't know if I'll have the strength to start it again!"

He didn't like it, but he nodded.

A sound escaped her that was half sob and half laugh. "It was a lie. Why it shocks me that he lied about that when he's been lying about everything else for years is something I just don't understand."

Carter had vanished into the house long enough to return with a blanket which he handed to Bennett. Bennett draped it over Mia's shoulders, but he wasn't even sure she'd noticed. Her gaze was distant, focused on the events of her past.

"She didn't leave to look for me," Mia said softly. "She left because she found out he was cheating. I know she knew before that. Everyone knew. But this one was different. It was someone she knew, someone she'd trusted. So she left the house, crying, screaming and upset and all this time, he let me think—*no*—he *made* me think it was my fault. That because of what I had done, I was responsible for taking care of her." She paused there for a moment, drawing in a deep shuddering breath. "So I did. I stayed. And I never told anyone because I felt so guilty, so ashamed of what I'd caused!"

It was diabolical and cruel. And it was typical Samuel Darcy. "I'm sorry, Mia. I'm so sorry for that."

"I found the letter today. The one that Mama's friend wrote to her confessing everything. Elizabeth Masters, née

Shelby, the caregiver was sent there by her whore of a mother to find it."

He closed his eyes. "The woman who almost killed you was in your house?"

"Yes. I don't blame her. I don't like her much, but I get it. She said the same thing to me last night. The one thing we had in common was a toxic fucking parent."

She looked up at him then and her gaze was focused and sharp. "I told him that I was done. That I was leaving. I didn't know where I would go. I thought Clayton and then maybe, if I was brave enough I'd try to talk to you. But then he got so mad because I wasn't bending to his will that he threw me out. I don't even have my driver's license. Or shoes."

Bennett glanced down at her bare feet. They were shredded and bloody from her walk. "Come inside, Mia."

"It was never because I didn't love you," she went on. The words just tumbled out of her. "I loved you more than anything, but he said that if I left, he'd put her in a home and that I'd never see her again. She would have died in one of those places, Bennett. I thought she was in that state because of my selfishness and if I left with you like I wanted, it would be even worse. She didn't deserve that. To be locked away and forgotten just because he couldn't be bothered to care for her, because I was selfish enough to put what I wanted ahead of her. There's no one to protect her, no one to make sure that she's taken care of if I don't do it!"

"No," he said. "She didn't deserve it. But neither did you." He didn't ask her to come inside again, but swept her up into his arms and carried her up the steps and into the house. Carter had already vanished, making himself scarce in the wake of big emotional scenes was right on target for him.

Bennett carried her to the bathroom and set her down on the edge of the tub just long enough to turn on the taps and let the water warm. "These grand entrances are making me an old man, Mia."

She chuckled, the sound watery and weak, but it was what he wanted to hear from her.

"I'm sorry," she whispered.

"For being dramatic?"

"For everything," Mia answered.

Bennett kneeled in front of her. "If it had been me, if I'd been sinking under the weight you've carried this long —I don't think I could have done it. But, Mia, I would have helped you."

"And then it would have been your guilt too. Do you honestly think that either of our eighteen-year-old selves could have lived with it and not turned on one another?" she demanded.

No. He didn't. There was nothing else to say to that. "Get those clothes off and get in the tub. You're half frozen. Savannah's got some clothes stashed around here somewhere. I'll find you something."

"I'll go to Clayton's once I can call him. I'm not here to put you on the spot. After last night—"

"You're not going anywhere tonight. You're going to take a bath, get warmed up, we'll take care of your feet, and then you're going to sleep. For as long as you need."

"I have to talk to Clayton. He's got to get Samuel out of that house and make sure that someone is there to take care of—"

"Mia! For fuck's sake! Get in the damn tub, and for once, trust me to take care of it...to take care of you."

She wilted in front of him. There was no other way to describe it. "I know you will," she finally said.

"Do not apologize or I will lose my shit," he said. "Bath. Now."

She nodded and he walked out of the room. He grabbed his phone off the table and called the only person he could think of. Matt answered after the second ring.

"Crawford."

"I need a cell number for Clayton Darcy."

"Am I a fucking search engine?"

Bennett closed his eyes. "Matt, this is not the time. It's about twenty kinds of crazy here right now and I need to talk to that asshole."

Matt sighed. "Fine."

Bennett listened to the sound of tapping keys. At any other time, he'd be giving Matt shit about making someone a great secretary, but at the moment his heart just wasn't in it.

Matt rattled off the number, and then added. "By the way, there's a pretty blonde in the waiting area outside of my office insisting that she talk to no one but me. She looks a hell of a lot like the chick from that picture."

"That's her sister, Elizabeth Masters. Maiden name was Shelby," Bennett supplied.

"Katherine Shelby. I'll be damned," Matt muttered. "She's the baby sister."

"She's a goddamn psycho who tried to kill Mia and then wormed her way into the house as a caregiver for Patricia."

"Right...so why's she here?"

Bennett sighed. "Right now, I can't tell you anything about the workings of a woman's mind. You want to know, ask her. She's apparently been in the mood to confess to a lot of things."

"Okay, then," Matt said. "I'll keep you posted."

"Thanks," Bennett said and ended the call. Elizabeth was the last of his concerns at the moment.

He dialed the number Matt had given him. When a male voice clicked on the other end, he said, "Clayton?"

"Yes."

"Bennett Hayes. Mia is at my house and will be for at least the next twenty-four hours. Your father is with Patricia, so you probably want to get somebody on that."

Clayton was quiet for a second. "Is Mia hurt?"

"Physically? No. I don't think so. But that son of a bitch is going to hell for the emotional shit he's put her through."

"That's an understatement. I know what he is, Hayes. I've known for a long time. I'm working on that, but taking down someone who is a professional liar like Samuel isn't easy."

Bennett said nothing for a moment, just let that simmer. "What do you need?"

"Something damaging enough to kill his social status. If he thinks he's losing that, he'll come to heel quick enough."

Bennett sighed. Mia wasn't the only one who'd been keeping a secret. "I need you to meet me at my brother's farm in an hour."

"Will I be leaving it alive?"

Bennett wasn't really sure how to answer that. Emmitt stayed to himself, practically a hermit. He liked it that way. And he hated the Darcys. All of them. "Alive, yes. Unscathed? Don't get out of your car unless I'm there."

"Fine," Clayton agreed.

Bennett ended that call as well. Standing in the middle of the living room, his phone in hand and his mind whirling with everything that had happened, he took a deep breath. After a couple of minutes, his brain still fogged and enough fury rolling inside him to kill Samuel Darcy with his bare hands, he went to the guest room and gathered up a T-shirt and pair of yoga pants that Savannah had left behind before heading to the too-quiet bathroom.

"Mia?" he called out. She didn't answer.

Bennett opened the door and found her sitting in the tub of water, half asleep. "Come on. Let's get you out of there."

"I'm not a child," she said, smacking at his hands.

"I'm looking at your naked body—no, you're damn well not. But you are asleep on your feet, or your ass at the moment anyway. So stop fighting me and let me help you."

"I don't think I know how," she answered honestly.

"Figure it out. I don't plan on stopping anytime soon," he shot back as he hauled her to her feet. Wrapping a towel around her, he walked her to the bedroom, his bedroom and ushered her inside.

"Just get under the covers. You can put these on later," he said. She was too tired even to dress herself. He could see her muscles trembling just from the effort of keeping herself upright. For once, she didn't argue. She climbed beneath the dark blue comforter and settled her head onto his pillow. He was pretty sure she was asleep before her body was even horizontal.

Heading back to the living room, he found Carter stealing his bag of chips and what was left of his beer. "You dickhead."

"Hey," Carter said, "I'm just getting out of your way."

"Don't. I need you to stay here with Mia while I take care of something," Bennett said.

"No. Oh, hell no. I do not deal with crying women."

"You made that pretty clear by running like a whipped dog at the sight of her!"

"I got her a blanket!" Carter protested. "That was sensitive."

Bennett closed his eyes and wondered, not for the first time, how many times Carter had hit his head on shit as a child. Since the things he'd hit the most had probably been Bennett's own fists, there wasn't much point in asking. "That was first aid, you dumb fuck!"

"How long?" Carter asked

"I don't know. An hour. Maybe two. She's going to sleep like the dead, she'll never even know I left."

"Fine. But you owe me."

"You've been paid in chips and beer," Bennett called back as he grabbed his keys and headed out. He had to beat Clayton Darcy to the farm or Emmitt might just put a bullet in him.

The Hayes family farm was on the outskirts of town, on the opposite end of Fontaine from the Fire Creek Distillery. Parking his car on the shoulder of the road just beyond the gate, Clayton was pretty sure that wasn't a coincidence.

Getting out of his car, he leaned against the door and waited for the approaching headlights to navigate all the hairpin turns of the tree lined gravel road.

It was Bennett's truck and as it pulled up, Clayton rose to his full height and waited for whatever was coming his way.

Bennett stopped his truck, climbed down and punched in the code to the gate. The chain link rolled away. "Go ahead," he said, "But don't even think about walking up to that door without me. Emmitt's not a big fan of people with your last name."

"I know the feeling," Clayton muttered, but as he climbed back into his car, there was no question that he would follow Bennett's advice. Emmitt Hayes was roughly the size of a mountain and looked like he lived on raw, potentially protesting, meat.

Once they were parked in front of the house, Bennett got out and climbed the steps, motioning for Clayton to stay where he was for the moment. He did, but he rolled down the window to hear every word.

After a second knock, lights came on in the house and Emmitt appeared at the door. "What the hell are you doing here?"

"What the hell were you doing in bed?" Bennett shot back.

"I worked last night," Emmitt replied. "Country vets don't keep city hours, jackass."

"Do you have the file on Darcy?" Bennett asked.

Emmitt looked past him at the car, and Clayton could tell by his look, that he recognized him immediately.

"What the fuck are you up to, Bennett?"

Bennett motioned for Clayton and reluctantly, he got out of his car and walked toward the porch. He remained at the foot of the steps, prepared to make a run for it if need be.

"We all have one thing in common," Bennett said. "Samuel Darcy has ruined the life of every person standing here."

Emmitt looked at him, and Clayton could feel the weight of his judgment. Standing there in his rumpled dress shirt, with his suit jacket still draped over the front seat, he was about as far apart from Emmitt Hayes and his dirty coveralls as another person could be.

"I doubt that," Emmitt said. "I'm not inviting a third-generation thief into my goddamn house, Bennett, and I'm sure as hell not giving him what we found."

Bennett cursed. "Emmitt, just listen for a damned minute, would you?"

"One minute," Emmitt agreed. "Make it count."

Bennett looked back at him and Clayton knew that if he didn't lay it all out, it would just be a waste of time. "Samuel ran Fire Creek into the ground. He borrowed against the company until it was so deep in the hole there was not getting it out. For years, he's been using it as his own private checking account, taking out money and never investing it back. We were on the brink of foreclosure when the three of us, Quentin, Mia and I, took all that we had, pooled it, and bought sixty percent of the company outright. Right now, I'm looking for anything I can use to make Samuel sign over the remaining forty and the house."

"Your family problems are no concern of mine," Emmitt said stiffly. "That whole damn place could burn to the ground, and I wouldn't even blink."

Clayton shrugged. "I never did anything to you, Emmitt. Not me. I've scoured every document in the archives. There's not a slip of paper that I haven't looked over to see if I could find a shred of proof that your great-grandfather had bought into Fire Creek. If it ever existed, it's gone now."

"Actually," Bennett interrupted. "It's not. We have it."

"What? Why the hell haven't you done anything with it?" Clayton demanded.

"The man wants to destroy his family business, let him," Emmitt answered. "We don't want it. The very idea of that place leaves a bad taste in my mouth. It destroyed our great-grandfather. Our grandfather lived like a beggar because of it, and our father died consumed with finding proof of it. I hate that damn place and I don't have a lot of love for its occupants."

"Emmitt," Bennet said cautiously. "I trust him. If we give him this, it gets us all something we want."

"What's that?"

"Freedom," Clayton replied. "It gets Samuel Darcy as far out of the picture as I can get him without digging him a grave. It gives Mia and Bennett a chance to make things right."

Emmitt looked at Bennett. "All this for that damned girl?"

"The *only* girl," Bennett answered. "But also, it's the right thing to do. Trust me, Emmitt."

Emmitt made a disgusted sound and slammed the door in their faces.

"That was an epic waste of time," Clayton stated.

Bennett didn't move, just stood there at the door. "Just wait for it."

A minute later, the door opened again and Emmitt shoved a heavy file folder at Bennett. "Do what you want with it. I'm tired of that shit taking up space."

The door slammed again, the lights went off, and they were left standing on the porch in the dark. "Is he always like that?"

"No," Bennett replied smoothly. "He was actually in a pretty good mood tonight."

Clayton shook his head in amazement. Storing that little nugget for another day, he glanced at the folder. "So what is all that?"

"Sworn affidavits, signed, witnessed, and notarized from the county clerk who was in office when, in 1962, your grandfather bribed him to make the original contract between him and our grandfather disappear. Your father was present."

"That's a thick folder for one document."

Bennett grinned. "That's only one thing your family did to ours. There's the property taxes that were only raised on our farm, courtesy of Samuel. There were the bank loans that would randomly come due because our payments weren't being applied to our loans. He held sway over this town because everyone here feared him. But they loved my father, and when he got sick, people came here of their own free will and gave him the evidence he'd been trying to gather his whole life."

"Does Mia know about this?" Clayton asked.

"Not yet. I'll tell her, but she's had a rough day. He lied to her about your mom's accident. He told her Patricia wrecked because she was out looking for Mia."

"While Mia was with you," Clayton finished. "Even if it were true, that's still not Mia's fault."

"Well, that's what she's been living with for the last ten years, with him putting that in her head every chance he got."

Clayton opened the back door of his car and pulled out an overnight bag. "I don't know what's in there. I called Evelyn and she went back to the house and packed for her while I escorted Samuel to his car."

Bennett grinned in the darkness. "I would have liked to see that."

"It was bloodless."

"Disappointing."

Yes, Clayton thought. It really was. He'd had to give up some of the information he'd accumulated in order to make it happen. It was a strategic concession, but it would complicate things in the future. Still, if it allowed Mia a chance at real peace and possibly even happiness, it would be worth it. "I'll check in with Mia tomorrow. I'm sure she needs the rest."

"I will look after her," Bennett reminded him.

"If I doubted that for a minute, I would have thrown you out of the hospital myself two weeks ago," Clayton reminded him.

Bennett pointed to the folder. "Whatever you do with all that, make it count."

"He's broke—flat fucking broke. He's living on credit that's about to be maxed out and mooching off friends who haven't quite figured it out yet," Clayton explained. "This was the final piece to force his hand."

"Into what?"

"Leaving. There's a ratty condo in Boca Raton with his name on it. If he wants to live in the lap of luxury, he's going to have to start dating twenty years older instead of just twenty years old."

Bennett laughed out loud. "That, I would actually pay to see, but only the G rated version. God above."

"Go take care of Mia," Clayton said. "I'll let you know how this shakes out."

Bennett nodded and climbed into his truck to drive away. Conscious of being alone and unarmed on Emmitt Hayes's property, Clayton got behind the wheel of his own vehicle and left quickly. He had a lot of work to do.

Nineteen

Mia awoke stiff, sore, and hungry. It was afternoon and judging from the nearly pristine condition of the bed around her, she hadn't moved since she laid down. Stretching, feeling every kink and every knotted muscle, she let out a groan.

"Oh, good! You're up."

Looking up, she saw Bennett's mother in the doorway. "Hi." This wasn't awkward. Not at all. She was naked in his bed on top of being the only daughter of their family's sworn enemy. Not to mention that most of his family probably had a pretty shitty opinion of her, too. There wasn't exactly an etiquette lesson on that kind of situation. *Sorry, I broke your son's heart a decade ago because my dad's a narcissistic asshole. Oh, and about that ugly scene on the lawn yesterday...*Yeah. Awkward.

Marianne smiled at her. "Come on down to the kitchen and I'll make you some breakfast. You have to be starving."

Mia's stomach chose that particular moment to growl. Loudly. "I am pretty hungry," she admitted. "I don't think I ate yesterday. And I'm a little fuzzy on the day before."

Marianne clucked her tongue. "We'll fix that. Give me about five minutes to get everything going."

The bedroom door closed and Mia let the sheet fall to her waist and buried her head in her hands. Her life had gone pretty much straight to hell. Okay, her life had changed lanes in hell. That was a better description.

Getting out of the bed, she found the clothes he'd left for her and quickly tugged them on. A glance in the mirror over his dresser revealed that her hair was a hopeless case. There were bruises on her arms, left by her father's grip. She had a good size knot on the back of her head, too. When they decided to take the gloves off, it had been literal.

Using her fingers, Mia tamed the mess of her hair the best she could and left the bedroom. Postponing the awkward conversation would not make it any better. Opening the bedroom door, she peered out and found the house deserted except for the sounds of pots and pans rattling in the kitchen. Even Slick was nowhere to be seen, though she had a vague recollection of him coming in and nuzzling her during the night. Hell, that could have been Bennett, for all she knew.

Entering the kitchen, Marianne was at the stove, scrambling eggs and frying bacon. It smelled like heaven.

Mia sat down at the counter. "Thank you for this."

"Don't thank me," she said. "It's the least I could do."

"It's a little more than that," Mia replied.

"You might rethink that after we talk," Marianne said.

Fuck. "I take it this is one of the *Come to Jesus* moments Bennett always talked about?"

"Hardly. Not having a penis, you can't be nearly as

hardheaded and stupid as a man. We can be a little more civil than that."

Mia chuckled in spite of herself. "Okay then, let's just have at it."

"Don't you want to eat first? It might ruin your appetite."

"Nothing could ruin my appetite right now," Mia said. "I might start chewing on a table leg in a minute."

"We can't have that," Marianne replied and placed a plate full of crisp bacon and fluffy scrambled eggs in front of her.

Mia immediately took a bite. It was as good as she'd hoped. She was still waiting for the other shoe to drop.

"I have never questioned, not one time, whether or not my son loved you. I never thought it was just the forbidden, tragic thing for him. I know Bennett straight to his soul and you, for better or worse, Mia Darcy, have marked him there." The other woman paused, and then cocked her head to the side in a considering way that was shockingly similar to her son. "But I have questioned whether or not you truly loved him."

Mia took a deep breath. "I think this is something that I need to talk to Bennett about first."

"Let me finish," Marianne said. "I questioned that until yesterday. I saw what it cost you. I heard what you've been carrying around all these years, and I heard something else, Mia. All that time, you carried it alone to save him from it. That's how I know you really love him."

Mia didn't have a response to that, so she just sat there silently and waited.

"My question now is whether or not you have the ability to let go of all that and make it work with him... because if you can't, you need to spare him the pain of losing you again."

"I don't know if he even wants that," Mia admitted.

"What do you want?" Marianne demanded.

Mia answered honestly. "Just him."

The older woman smiled. "Your brother brought Bennett some of your things last night. I don't know what they're cooking up together but I can't imagine it's anything but trouble. Finish your breakfast, get yourself cleaned up, and when he walks into this house, you show him you're not broken. You don't need him to be your hero. You just need *him*."

Marianne walked out and Mia just sat and stared after her. One day, she was going to grow up to be that woman, she thought. Gracious and composed, unflinchingly honest. For the time being however, she was going to have to fake it.

Finishing her meal, she grabbed the bag and went back to the small bathroom to get herself in some semblance of order. Shampooing and conditioning her hair was the first order of business. With that done, she combed it out and left it loose to dry. There wasn't a flat iron in her bag, but Evelyn, lord bless her, was clueless about those things. Thankfully, her makeup bag had been tossed in.

By the time she heard the front door opening, she was dressed in her own clothes, made up and feeling at least somewhat like herself. Heading down the hallway, she found Bennett in the kitchen.

"I wondered if you'd still be here," he said.

"I'm sort of homeless now," she replied jokingly.

Bennett reached into his back pocket and produced a thick envelope stuffed with papers. "Not really."

Mia opened the envelope and scanned the contents. The house, her parents' house, had been deeded to her.

"How did he do this? What did you and Clayton do?" she demanded.

"It was mostly Clayton. He already had enough ammunition on your dad to pretty much get what he wanted out of him. I just handed him the smoking gun."

"And that was?"

"Proof that at one time, Fire Creek had belonged to both of our great-grandfathers, and that at the time of my great-grandfather's death, your grandfather and father together, bribed the local officials to destroy the contracts and records—which they did, except for one."

"You own part of my family's distillery," she whispered in amazement.

"No," he said emphatically. "None of us want that. I don't. Emmitt sure as hell doesn't. The distillery is a one hundred percent Darcy enterprise and that's how it's going to stay."

"So why all the research? Why track down the evidence?"

"That was mostly Emmitt," Bennett said. "It was for Dad. He needed the proof. And before he died, people brought it to him. It gave him peace...us too, I guess."

Mia sighed. "Well, you all have a partnership in a distillery you don't want, and now I have a house I don't want."

Bennett sat down at the counter, settling into the same chair she'd vacated earlier. "What do you want, Mia?"

"You," she said, "are the second person to ask me that today. The answer is always the same. Just you."

He reached for her, taking her hands and tugging her close until she had no choice but to sprawl across his lap. "What about the house...your mother? There's lots of things to figure out."

"There are," she agreed. "And for the first time in our lives, we'll have the time."

"I still have your ring—the one I bought all those years ago. And some day, maybe soon, when we're both ready, I will put that damn thing on your finger."

She kissed him, savoring the moment, the freedom to do so without any fear of reprisal. "And one day soon, when we're both ready, I'll let you. I just want to enjoy this. I want to walk down Main Street with you. I want to go to movies and dance and do all the things we never got to do because people might see."

He looped his arms more tightly around her and held on. "This is it, Mia. This time, it's really ours."

"In that case, do you really want to be sitting here in this kitchen when you have a perfectly good bed down the hall?"

"I never stopped loving you," he admitted. "I prayed that I would, like I have never prayed for anything else."

"So did I," she admitted. "And right now, I've never been happier that a prayer wasn't answered. I love you, Bennett. Finally, I can shout it from the rooftops if I want."

He rose, picked her up in his arms and strode down the hall toward his room. "You can do that later. I've got a different kind of screaming I want to hear from you right now."

She laughed at that. "You can have anything you want, as long as I can have you."

Epilogue

ONE YEAR LATER...

Bennett Hayes walked through the doors of the Fire Creek Distillery and all heads turned. It was still an odd thing. A Hayes walking into the Darcy family business and no one shouting for security or calling the cops. After all, family feuds in the Bluegrass State tended to be of epic proportion. But those days were over. With Samuel Darcy's toxic ass gone from the town of Fontaine and out of the lives of his children, they were all finally at peace—even if they didn't know what the hell to make of it.

"Hayes!"

Bennett looked up to see Mia's older brother, Clayton Darcy, making a beeline for him. That wasn't good. They might have called a truce but they'd never be friends. "Clayton," Bennett acknowledged.

The eldest Darcy sibling stopped directly in front of him. "Do me a favor and don't leave big ass hickeys on my baby sister before we have important board meetings. In fact, just don't leave big ass hickeys on her at all. I don't need the visual confirmation of what y'all do when I'm not around."

Bennett didn't say anything in response to that. Informing Clayton that he had a matching bite mark in a well concealed location would not make anything better. Instead he just ignored the whole thing. "Is Mia in her office?"

"She is," Clayton replied. "And you all are expected this weekend for Emma Grace's birthday party. Two o'clock at the Pizza Spot. Don't be late."

Bennett nodded as he walked away, heading straight for Mia's office. The smell of sour mash filled the air in the distillery. There wasn't a Kentuckian alive who didn't know that particular aroma and got a little misty eyed over it. And for his money, there was no better bourbon around than Fire Creek. Even when the very name Darcy had made him cringe, he'd still taken a nip or two of the product from time to time.

With a sharp knock, he opened the door to Mia's office and stepped inside. She was in the middle of a conference call, smiling into the camera on her laptop and looking like the Southern royalty she was. Just out of frame, she held up one finger to shush him and simultaneously let him know she was almost done.

It took another minute or so for her to wrap up the call and shut everything down. Then she leaned back in her chair, stretched and let out a tired groan as she rolled her neck from side to side. "Remind me to tell you no the next time you decide to get amorous in the middle of the week."

Bennett grinned. "That was all you. I was just lying in bed minding my own business and you had to walk in dressed like every fantasy I've ever had since I was a seven-teen-year-old boy—"

"I was wearing a T-shirt!" Mia protested.

"Like I said, every fantasy I've ever had since I was a boy," he doubled down. "Now, get your purse. I've got a surprise for you."

"I can't just leave. It's only four in the afternoon."

"You can. Your last name is Darcy, Mia. That does come with some perks," he pointed out. "Let's go. The truck's running."

She sighed but grabbed her purse just the same. Slipping the strap over her shoulder, she rose from her desk. "You're a bad influence on me, Bennett Hayes."

"Wouldn't be the first time," he said, ushering her out the office door with a smack on her perfectly curved behind. There were a million and one things he loved about her body, but her ass was truly perfect. And if things went the way he hoped they would, that luscious behind would be his for life.

They were in Bennett's truck. She had scooted all the way to the middle and was seated right beside him. He had one arm thrown around her shoulders and the other hand on the wheel. It was a perfect moment—perfect in the present and a perfect representation of their past. How many times had she sat in the front seat of his beat-up old car, pressed to his side with his arm slung around her and some obnoxious music on the radio? Even thinking about it made her smile.

"What's that for?" he asked.

"The past. The present. Us," she mused. "It's good, isn't it? Where we are now?"

He looked at her strangely for just a moment, shadows in his eyes that hadn't been there just a minute before. "Is this all you want, Mia? Just the present? Just the memories of our past? What about the future?"

Her heart did that funny little skip that always happened whenever they started to talk about the future. She was afraid to want it. Afraid that if she let herself think too much about it, it would all disappear again. "Let's not borrow trouble, Bennett."

He eased the truck off the highway and onto the gravel road that would lead to the springhouse. She should have known that when he said he had a surprise for her it would involve their spot. It had always been their spot. Every day after school they'd slipped away and spent hours there. Sometimes it had been innocent—sweet, even. Other times it had been heated and sensual.

When the truck rolled to a stop and Bennett climbed out, she waited patiently for him to come around and open the door for her. It would have been easier to just get out. But he liked to do those things for her, and she secretly enjoyed it.

When the door opened and he took her hand to help her out, she smiled at him. As her heels sank into the dirt, she pressed a kiss to his cheek. "I love you, Bennett."

His expression remained tight. "I'll remind you of that shortly. Let's get inside. It's cold as shit out here."

The truck door slammed as she walked away from it. Bennett took a couple of quick steps and was once more at her side. At the door to the springhouse, he pulled a set of keys from his pocket and within seconds, the padlock sprang free and he removed it from the latch, slipping it into his pocket. When he pulled the door open, Mia was not prepared for what she saw. Inside, the old wooden building had been transformed. Strings of light had been draped from the ceiling. In the far corner, a nest of blankets and pillows had been created for them.

"Did Savannah help you with this?" she asked.

He looked at her balefully. "I am capable of completing a romantic gesture without asking for my sister's expertise."

"Those pillows are from the international market and cost half the earth, Bennett."

"I borrowed them from her," he said. "Now, hush before you ruin it."

Mia laughed and made a production of zipping up her lips before stepping deep into the springhouse. Beneath the wooden floor, she could hear the gurgling of the stream that had been the sole purpose of the building's existence at one point.

Next to the nest of silk blankets and embroidered velvet pillows was a tote bag from her favorite restaurant in Lexington. "Did you get fried chicken from the Merrick Inn? And chocolate cake?"

He grinned. "Of course, I did. What else would I get from there?"

A bucket of champagne was chilling as well. "Did I forget an anniversary?" The feeling of panic was intense. Bennett was so much better about that sort of thing than she was.

"No. It's not an anniversary—not yet, anyway."

Mia turned to him then. "All right, I'm getting nervous. What's going on, Bennett?"

"I had this whole scene planned," he admitted ruefully. "I was going to ply you with good food, then kiss you until you were nothing but a boneless heap. But I forgot for a minute about your suspicious nature and unwillingness to take anything at face value."

She just nodded, waiting for further explanation. When he dropped to one knee in front of her and pulled a small black velvet box from his jacket pocket, her heart began to race in her chest, beating like the entire drumline of a marching band. "Bennett?"

Bennett, with his eyes shining with all the love he had for her, held up the ring—the same ring he'd been holding on to for all those years. "We've waited long enough, haven't we? Ten years apart and I never stopped loving you. Never stopped wanting you, and for the last year we've been existing in the moment—just one to the next. Both of us too afraid to reach out for more. But I don't want just a moment, Mia. I want forever. I want to know that all the minutes going forward are minutes that we'll share."

She wasn't even aware of the tears that flowed freely down her face. "Bennett..."

"Don't tell me no. Tell me you need more time. Tell me you need to think. Tell me anything you want to except no. Just don't tell me no."

"Yes," she whispered. "Of course, it's a yes. I've never wanted anything else as much as I want that. Since I was too young to even know what being someone's wife meant, that's all I ever wanted to be."

Mia didn't know if it was his hands that were shaking or her own as he slid the ring over her finger. The weight of it was both comforting and terrifying. When it was settled firmly at the base of her finger, the diamond winking in the light, she sank to her knees in front of him.

"I love you. I love you so much, Bennett. I cannot wait to be Mia Darcy-Hayes. I'd marry you tomorrow if I could."

He pulled back, looking at her strangely for just a moment. "No big wedding?"

"No. I don't care about any of that. I just want to be your wife." It was true. Mia had never meant anything more.

Bennett grinned. "Well, I happen to know that there's this grocery store across the state line in Tennessee. It worked out pretty well for Carter and Josie."

That grin of his was her undoing. Every single time. It took him from gorgeous to god-like and she had never been able to resist it. "Fine. I don't care. As long as it's legal and binding, but I'm not your wife yet, Bennett. Tonight is the last night on earth that we get to have sex like we're just dating. You think maybe you could take those pants off and we could commit a few sins before we're protected by the sanctity of marriage?"

She didn't have to ask twice.

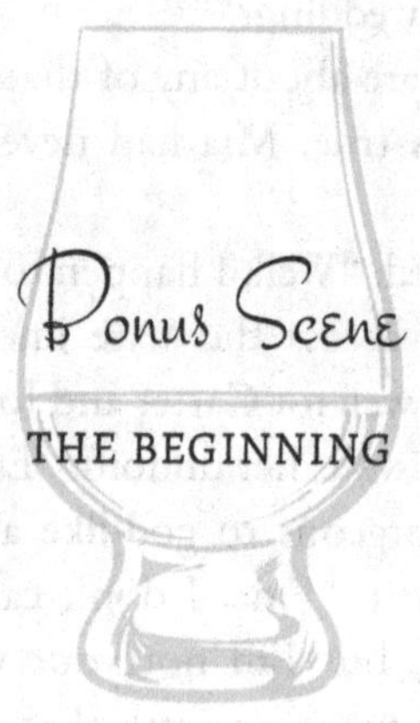

Bonus Scene

THE BEGINNING

TEN YEARS AGO...

The house was quiet, but then it was always quiet, Mia reflected. Since her mother's accident, Quentin never came home and Clayton was enthralled with his fiancée. She rarely saw either one of them. Her father made the rare appearance, but by and large it was just her in the house with the nurses and aides who cared for Patricia.

Strolling aimlessly through her room, Mia allowed her fingers to trail over the furniture, the toys that she hadn't yet put away, the awards and trophies she'd earned over the years. Everything would be left behind and she didn't know when she would ever see those things again. She was excited and terrified all at the same time.

Moving to the bed, Mia lay back and stared up at the ceiling. Her heart was pounding in her chest and she was practically trembling with nerves. On the one night when she needed to be alone in the house, when she needed her father to be his typical absentee self, he was ensconced in the family room, drinking bourbon and watching a basketball game she couldn't imagine he cared about one way or another.

Glancing at the clock on the bedside table, she felt the first stirrings of true panic. She was supposed to meet him at the spring house in fifteen minutes. As it was, she'd already be late. Waiting for Samuel to leave was no longer an option. She'd have to sneak past him.

Eloping with Bennett Hayes was, in her family, at least, a hanging offense. It was something Samuel would never forgive, but then she had her fair share of grudges against him too. They were dysfunctional to say the least. But it wasn't about pissing off her father; it wasn't even about rebelling against the overwhelming expectations placed on her by virtue of being a Darcy. It was just about him, about the way he made her feel.

She'd known of him her whole life, but they'd gone through school together without even speaking to one another. No one questioned it. Teachers made sure they sat far apart or were in different classrooms altogether. It was understood that anyone with the names Hayes and Darcy were to be kept as far apart as possible. That had worked until the party Loralei had thrown when her parents were in Europe.

It was the first time they'd ever spoken, and it was simply magical. He was sweet and funny, and he made her feel like she wasn't just the prettiest girl in the world, he made her feel like she was the only one.

Bennett was the best thing that had ever happened to her and she wasn't going to let him go just because her asshole of a father didn't like his last name. The Hayes and Darcy families had been feuding for so long half of them didn't even know why. Regardless, she wasn't going to let that, or the quaking fear that she felt at the thought of tangling with her father over him, stop her from being with him.

Thinking about the night he'd asked her to marry him, Mia smiled. He'd opened that velvet box and showed her the ring. They both knew she couldn't wear it, that it would cause too many questions. But she'd said yes without even hesitating. He'd slipped it on her finger, and it had been the most blissful moment of her life. She'd given it back to him as she left that night, and he'd promised her that the next time he put a ring on her finger, it would be there to stay.

"It's now or never," she whispered to herself.

With shaking hands and knees that were none too steady, Mia rose and grabbed the single overnight bag that she was taking with her. Her other things were already in the car. She'd been sneaking out a piece or two at a time and packing them into trash bags in her car for the last two weeks.

Moving as silently as possible, she crept down the back stairs and into the kitchen. When she reached the little plaque with its row of hooks that hung by the back door, she stopped dead in her tracks. Her keys weren't there.

"Looking for these?"

She could hear the sneer in her father's voice before she even turned around to face him. "Why do you have my car keys?" It was a rhetorical question. They both knew that. He wouldn't be there, he wouldn't have taken her keys if he didn't suspect something. Asking him was just a way of buying time, delaying the inevitable.

He smiled, though it was a cold and chilling expression. "A better question might be why you need them at nine o'clock at night. Just where do you think you're going, Mia?"

"I was going to stay with Loralei," she lied. It was a familiar tale. She'd spun it often enough over the last year, and Loralei, God bless her, had covered for her every time.

Samuel slammed his hand down on the counter with enough force to rattle every dish in the kitchen and Mia jumped. She'd seen his temper before, but never directed at her. For the most part, she'd gone her whole life without even really gaining his attention.

"Don't lie to me, girl! You were going to meet him!"

Dread filled her, but she elected to brazen it out. "I don't know what you're talking about."

"Bennett Hayes, Amelia!" he shouted, reverting to her full name, which they both hated. "I have turned a blind eye to your cavorting with him because I assumed it was a phase and that you would eventually recognize him for the trash he is."

"Trash?" she questioned. "The only thing the Hayes family is guilty of is not bowing and scraping to you because you're an almighty Darcy!"

He swept his arm over the counter and the ceramic bowl on the counter went crashing to the floor. It shattered and the odds and ends it always seemed to collect, rather than the fruit it was intended for, scattered over the tiles.

"I've raised you to be a lot of things, but a liar isn't one of them!"

She laughed. "You haven't raised me at all! You were barely here!"

"So that's what this is all about?" he scoffed. "You wanted my attention, Mia? Now you've got it. You're a spoiled, ungrateful, selfish brat. I've given you everything and you repay me by whoring yourself out to our sworn enemy?"

"I'm not going to stand here and listen to this," she said. "Give me my keys!"

He closed his fist over the keys and glared at her. "They're not yours! That car, this house, the clothes on your back. I paid for every damn bit of it. You own nothing, little girl, except what I see fit to give you."

There was no way it was going to end well. He wouldn't accept anything less than ugliness. Taking the overnight bag off her shoulder, she put it on the counter. She reached into her purse and took out her driver's license and the cash she had on hand before dropping the designer bag onto the counter along with her other things.

"The money is mine. I earned it working at the distillery this summer. You can keep everything else," she said and turned toward the door.

"You're not even going to bother denying it, are you?" he sneered, his tone scathing and accusatory. "After everything that you've put this family through with your self-ishness, you're not even going to hesitate to run off with him!"

The fury that swept through her was shocking. She hated her father and had hated him for a very long time. The string of affairs, the way he lorded his wealth over other people, the fact that he used everyone for his own ends—she couldn't stand the sight of him. But in that moment, with that accusation weighing on her, she could have killed him.

She spun around, shouting at the top of her lungs. "What I've put this family through? Me? What about you and all that you've done? My mother's life was a misery because of you!"

His eyes glittered coolly as he replied, "And now it isn't even that because of you. Where do you think she was going that night, Mia? Why do you think your mother, who hated to drive in the rain, was out on these winding roads at night in a storm?"

Mia didn't answer, just whirled and reached for the door handle.

"She called Loralei's mother to check up on you all," he continued softly. "Imagine how surprised she was to find out that Loralei was grounded and not allowed to have company and that you, her precious angel, had lied to her."

Mia stood there, her hand hovering over the knob. "I'm not listening to your lies."

"Why would I lie? I've tried to protect you from the ugly truth, to shield you from the knowledge that your selfishness caused your mother's accident, that she's just a shell of the woman she once was and it's all because of your thoughtless actions."

"No," she whispered, fighting the tears that threatened. "That isn't true."

"You know it is, Mia. Deep down, you've known all along. Why else would she go out in the storm, after dark? What reason, other than for one of her children, would she have braved such conditions?"

She couldn't breathe. The weight of his words crushed her, squeezing the air from her lungs. On the heels of the shock came the guilt. It clawed at her, twisting and pulling inside her until she thought she would break from it. "I don't believe it," she whispered. She was lying to herself as much as she was lying to him in that moment.

"And if your brothers learned the truth," he continued, "they might forgive you in time. But would you ever forgive yourself for robbing them of the mother they adored?"

Bile rose in her throat. Her stomach churned and her head was spinning with it all. Even then, she recognized that he was enjoying it. Exerting his will, making her bend to him, stroked his massive ego. "I hate you." As softly as the words were uttered, the power of the naked honesty behind them was unmistakable.

"Hate me all you want, but know this, Mia. If you walk out that door, if you run off with that white trash, you will never see your mother again. I will take her from this house, I will put her in a home, and you will not be allowed near her. Do you understand me?"

"I understand," she said.

"How long do you think Patricia would survive in a place like that?" he asked coolly.

She wouldn't. Mia knew that. So did he. If she left and allowed him to put her mother in a place like that, it would be a death warrant for her. Unsure of how much of her mother actually remained in the frail body just a few yards away, Mia accepted in that moment that he'd won. She would give up what she wanted, what she needed, to do what she should.

Mia didn't say anything. She couldn't. But her hand slipped from the doorknob and she turned back toward him. Gathering her things, she moved past him and climbed the stairs toward her room. Each step took more effort. With each one, she felt heavier and more weighted down by what he'd just placed on her shoulders.

When she reached her room, Mia picked up the phone and called the only person she could think of who would help her. Clayton answered after the third ring. "What is it?"

"I need you to come home," she said, and couldn't stop her voice from trembling or the tears that rolled freely down her cheeks.

"Is it Mama?" he asked and the panic in his voice only caused her to cry harder.

"No. Mama's fine. I didn't mean to scare you. But, Clayton, I need you here. He'll come here and if he does, Samuel will kill him!"

"Who will, Mia?" he asked, his voice soothing and patient as only he could be.

"Bennett," she whispered. "I was supposed to leave with him tonight, but I can't. And when he comes here to find out why, I don't even want to think about what Samuel will do."

She heard his answering sigh and the soft murmur of a feminine voice in the background. Then he answered. "It'll take me a while to get there. I'm at Annalee's apartment and with the game, the traffic downtown is awful, but I'll be there as soon as I can."

"Thank you," she said.

Clayton paused before hanging up. He wasn't speaking but she could hear the background noise and the music playing. When he did speak, the question was couched very carefully. "Do you want to go with him, Mia?"

"I can't," she replied. It was the most honest answer she could give. "I just can't, that's all."

Bennett eased the ancient Buick up the driveway of the Darcy home. *Estate.* It wasn't just a house. It was two hours past the time Mia had been supposed to meet him and an hour past the time he'd accepted that she wasn't coming. A part of him wanted to go home, to forget it and to forget her. Another part of him insisted that something must have gone wrong. Samuel Darcy wasn't known to be violent, but he wasn't known to be merciful either.

So there he sat, parked in the circular drive in front of her house with every ounce of pride he possessed ripped to shreds. He took a deep breath and got out, the car door creaking loudly.

For the first time in his life, Bennett didn't sneak onto the property. He wasn't hiding in the shadows and slipping into her room under the cover of darkness. Climbing the steps, he marched straight to the front door and rang the bell. It was a bad idea. Even in his anger and his fear, he knew it was a bad idea, but it goaded him more than a little to be the thing that she had to hide. He'd always hated feeling like she was ashamed of him, even if he understood that it wasn't really that at all. The Hayes pride was a fucking curse.

The door opened and Samuel Darcy greeted him. "You get the hell off my property, boy, or I will end you."

Bennett stood his ground, even if it was the dumbest damn thing he'd ever done in his life. "I'm not going anywhere until I see Mia."

"That's not going to happen. You've got until I count to ten and then I'm putting a bullet in you."

Bennett backed up, but didn't leave. Looking up at the dimly lit windows of the second floor, specifically the one on the far right as he knew it was Mia's room, he called out. "Mia! I need to talk to you!"

The only response was the light in her room flicking off, the window going black.

"She doesn't want anything to do with you," Samuel said.

"Why are you even here?" Bennett asked. "You never stay at this house...why tonight of all nights, are you here?"

Samuel pulled the pistol from his belt. "You don't question me in my own goddamn house!"

Bennett was too angry, too hurt to care. "What did you threaten her with to make her back out?"

"I didn't have to threaten her!" Samuel shouted back. "She came to her senses and decided she didn't want to live in a goddamn trailer park with the likes of you!"

Bennett's fists were clenched at his sides. "It takes a big fucking man to say that hiding behind a gun."

Another car pulled up, and Bennett glanced over his shoulder to see Clayton Darcy walking toward him. He was outnumbered and was probably going to get his ass handed to him.

"I need to see your sister."

Clayton looked at him for a moment, as if silently weighing his options, before finally speaking. "She doesn't want to see you. You need to leave."

God, that fucking hurt. It was like having his skin peeled off. "I'd like to hear that from her."

Clayton moved toward him, slowly, menacingly. Bennett knew he was strong, but he was a hell of a lot skinnier and a couple of inches shorter than Mia's brother. Those things mattered in a fight, and he didn't doubt for a second they were going to have one.

"You're leaving," Clayton warned. "Either on your own or because I make you. Don't do this the hard way."

Bennett heard the pity in the other man's voice. That pissed him off more than anything. "Fuck you."

Clayton sighed, even as he threw the first punch. Bennett ducked to the side, the blow glancing off his cheekbone as he tossed a punch of his own. It caught him in the gut but didn't seem to faze him at all.

They traded blows, eventually winding up grappling on the porch floor. Struggling for control, fighting like his life depended on it, Bennett rolled and they were just close enough to the edge of the porch to roll right off the steps. His head hit the bottom step, the rough brick taking a chunk of flesh right at his hairline and nearly knocking him senseless. The grass was cold on his back as he struggled to regain his footing, but it was too late. Clayton was standing over him. He grasped Bennett's shirt and hauled him up, only to send his fist crashing into Bennett's face.

"Don't get up," Clayton urged softly. "For the love of God, just stay down. If you get up again, that son of a bitch will shoot you."

Bennett's head rolled to the side and he saw Samuel standing on the porch, his pistol ready. There was still no sign of Mia. "He made her do this," Bennett protested.

"If you get up again," Clayton said, "it had better be to walk away. She doesn't want you here and she's not going with you. That's all you need to know. It was her choice."

The truth was an ugly thing, but Bennett heard it then. Clayton was right. Maybe Samuel was the reason, but the choice had been Mia's. She'd chosen to back out, and she'd chosen the coward's way out and wouldn't even face him to tell him herself.

"You can all go to hell," he said as he stumbled to his feet and toward his waiting car. He hated them all in that moment.

Clayton watched the younger man walk away and it went against everything in him. He'd known about Mia and Bennett. He'd let it go, electing not to interfere. Now both of them were heartbroken and he was just as much to blame as Samuel was.

He climbed the steps toward the house, wincing. The kid might have been skinny, but he punched like a damn kicking mule.

"I should have shot him," Samuel said.

Clayton ignored him and walked into the house. Mia was huddled on the stairs, her eyes red and her face wet with tears.

"Jesus fucking Christ," Clayton muttered and ran his hands through his hair. "Mia, I just had to beat the shit out of that boy for no good reason other than having the idiocy to get tangled up with this family. What the hell is going on?"

Mia didn't answer him. Instead, she looked past him to Samuel who'd just come in and locked the door. When she did look at him, her face was a carefully schooled mask, her eyes blank and not a spark of life in her. "I changed my mind. I realized I was making a terrible mistake and I couldn't face him to tell him the truth."

It was a lie. Clayton knew it the minute she uttered the words. Mia had never been afraid to face anything as far as he knew. If she was afraid, it had to be huge. "Mia, if you wanted to be with him—"

"I can't be with him," she stated emphatically. "I can't. It was foolish of me to ever think otherwise."

"Damn straight," Samuel said, all swagger and ego. "There's never been a Hayes born that was worthy of a Darcy."

"We're not so special," she said. "You're a middle-aged cliché and our family has been dysfunctional from day one."

Samuel's expression soured, his lips firming into a thin, hard line. "He's not of our class, Mia. You could and will do much better, once this infatuation fades."

A bitter laugh escaped her, and she stared at their father, clearly as dumbfounded by his ego as Clayton was.

"You might be able to stop me from being with Bennett," she stated, with steel in her voice, "but you can't make me want to be with someone else. Just get out. Go to whatever cheap, tawdry whore you're keeping these days and stop pretending to be a father who cares. It's the only kind of lying you don't excel at."

She had been pushed to the breaking point and Clayton knew it. Deciding to intervene again, he opened the door for their father and gestured for him to leave. "You've done enough damage. You can leave any time now."

"As soon as my back is turned, she'll be running off with that trash," Samuel said smugly.

Mia rose and walked to the door. Bennett's taillights were fading in the distance, so far down the road she could barely make them out anymore. "I'm not going anywhere," Mia said softly. "He wouldn't want me now anyway...not after this. You've won."

Mia turned on her heel and made her way up the stairs, leaving Clayton and her father to stare after her. There were no words to describe what she felt. The storm of emotions inside her—guilt, grief, anger, and the utter hopelessness of it all—was overwhelming.

She reached the relative sanctuary of her room and stood there in the middle of it, uncertain of what to do next. Her only plan for her life had been to be halfway to Tennessee by midnight and married by morning. Now that was gone. Samuel had taken everything away and left her instead with a guilt so fierce she felt like it was eating her alive.

She heard the footsteps and knew that it was Clayton, always the overprotective brother, coming to check on her. He knocked on the door but didn't wait for her to answer. It was just as well. She was incapable. If she opened her mouth to speak, she'd scream and never stop.

"Are you okay?" he asked.

Mia nodded.

"Liar," he accused softly. "What did he do, Mia? What is that son of a bitch holding over your head?"

That question would require more than a nod. Forcing herself to speak, to rein in the misery inside of her, Mia answered, "It doesn't matter. Bennett and I probably wouldn't have worked anyway. We're night and day in every way that matters."

"Except that you're both clearly crazy about one another, and have been for the last year. Did you honestly think I didn't know?"

Yes. She had truly believed she was being that discreet. Apparently she'd failed miserably. Changing the subject, she asked the thing that she dreaded. "How badly did you hurt him?"

Clayton shrugged. "I'd say he gave as good as he got. The bottom step did him in more than me. Thank God for it. I'd hate to have my ass kicked by a skinny eighteen-year-old."

Mia smiled because she knew she was supposed to. "I know you had to hurt him to make him leave. Thank you for helping me. I couldn't do it," she admitted. "I couldn't look at him and tell him that I—" She stopped, unable to finish the sentence.

"Couldn't tell him what, Mia?" Clayton demanded.

I destroyed our family. I destroyed our mother. My selfishness has robbed her of any semblance of life and robbed you and Quentin of her. And I'm too much of a coward to be honest with any of you. Mia pressed her forehead to the glass. She couldn't bring herself to tell him the truth. "It doesn't matter. Thank you for coming. For helping me."

"I'll always help you. But right now, you're not helping yourself a whole lot. He'd forgive you. It might take a while—"

"No," Mia said. "That's over now. It has to be. Samuel would make his life a misery, his entire family would be targeted, you know how he operates. Petty, vindictive, mean. It was stupid of me to ever think we could get away with this."

"Do you love him?" Clayton asked.

"No," she lied.

Clayton sighed, accepting her lie while clearly not believing it. "Samuel is gone, but I'm staying here tonight...I'm worried about you."

"I'm okay," she said. "I will be, anyway. You can go back to Annalee. I know I dragged you away from her."

He just shook his head. "Get some sleep, Mia. I'll see you in the morning. Everything will look better then."

No, it wouldn't. But she didn't bother to correct him. When the door closed behind him, she sank down on her bed, a bed that she had shared with Bennett more times than she could count. But he'd never again sneak in through her bedroom window. He'd never hold her close while she slept.

Mia didn't cry. She was afraid that if she started to cry again, she'd never stop. Instead, she lay down on the bed and closed her eyes, willing herself to sleep. It was the only escape she had at the moment.

Bennett didn't go home. If his mother saw him in his current state, it wouldn't go over well. Instead, he drove the short distance to his grandmother's house. She lived on the same road as the Darcys, less than two miles from them. It was a little more than half a mile going through the woods. Not that he'd ever be doing that again.

Getting out of the car, his whole body hurt. Clayton Darcy had about seven years on him, and about thirty pounds more of muscle. Every punch had felt like being hit by a truck. With his lip split, his eye blacked and more than a couple of bruised ribs, Bennett could admit that he'd had his ass handed to him. But he'd landed a few good licks, as well. Clayton's lip was split too, and he'd be sporting a few bruises of his own.

Climbing the steps to his grandmother's porch, he let himself in. The door wasn't locked. It never was. Carter was sitting on the couch, eating chips and drinking a suspiciously colored soda. But they'd been adding ill-gotten liquor to their soft drinks for years. It was sneaky but it worked.

"What the fuck happened to you?"

"Carter Emanuel Hayes! Watch your mouth!"

The admonition had come from the kitchen, where his grandmother was probably making a plate for him already. No one came to her house that they didn't immediately get fed.

"Clayton Darcy beat the shit out of me," Bennett replied and plucked the bottle from Carter's hand. He took a long swig, and the vodka-laced soda burned like fire going down.

"That's not exactly how tonight was supposed to go," Carter replied.

Bennett eased himself down on the vinyl recliner that had been his grandfather's. "She didn't show. And when I went to the house to find out why, Samuel threatened to shoot me, and Clayton beat my ass."

She doesn't want you here, and she's not going with you. That's all you need to know. The words reverberated in his mind like an echo in a canyon. They just went on forever.

Carter didn't say anything for a long time. "Well, that sucks," he finally offered, a lame attempt at empathy.

If it wouldn't have hurt every bone in his body to do so, Bennett would have laughed. "Yeah. I'm going to bed before Nana comes in and sees my face. Tomorrow morning is early enough to explain it all," Bennett said. As an afterthought, he reached into his pocket and pulled out the velvet box. "Get rid of that."

"What the hell am I going to do with an engagement ring?" Carter demanded.

"Sell it, pawn it, throw it in the darkest goddamn hole in this town," Bennett said. "I don't care."

Bennett didn't see Carter slip the ring in his pocket, he was already halfway up the stairs and heading to the same small bedroom he always used when he stayed at his nana's house. He wanted to be angry, or heartbroken, or any of the other things he thought he ought to feel. Instead, he just felt tired and confused.

As he laid down, he thought of Mia, of the promises they'd made to one another. There was no backup plan. He hadn't thought beyond marrying her, beyond running away from Fontaine and starting a life with her. What the hell was he supposed to do now?

"Goddamn the Darcys," he muttered in the darkness. He wanted to hate her, but it just wasn't in him. But he'd be damned if he'd beg for her. He knew what it was to miss someone, and he knew what it meant to get up and get on with his life anyway. He'd watched his mother do that after his father died, and it wasn't in him to do any different. It would hurt like hell, but he'd get used to it and eventually, he'd stop noticing it at all.

Bennett rolled over onto his side and stared out at the night sky. The moon was full and there wasn't a cloud in sight. He'd be okay, he knew that. It wasn't how he wanted things to end, but he'd get through it. He wasn't sure about her, and that bothered him more than he cared to admit.

"It's not your problem to fix," he said aloud. Maybe, if he told himself that often enough, he'd believe it. He couldn't save Mia from herself, and he wasn't going to lose himself trying to. It was over and he'd move on.

A Look At

CIARAN

A BOURBON & BLOOD NOVELLA

She trusted him with her heart. Now she has to trust him with her life.

Ciaran Darcy knows he doesn't deserve Loralei Crawford. Their fiery romance ended in heartbreak when he pushed her away, convinced he'd never fit into her privileged world. But when Loralei becomes the target of a ruthless criminal seeking revenge against her brother, Ciaran is the only one with the skills to keep her safe.

Thrown back into each other's lives, the sparks between them reignite—but so do the doubts and fears that tore them apart. Loralei isn't sure she can trust the man who broke her heart, even as danger closes in around her. For Ciaran, protecting Loralei isn't just about keeping her alive—it's about proving he's the man she needs by her side.

With time running out and the past threatening to destroy their future, can they find their way back to each other—or will their second chance slip away forever?

AVAILABLE APRIL 2025

Chasity Bowlin is a *USA Today* bestselling author of numerous romance novels. She resides in central Kentucky with her husband, their charming son, and a lively menagerie of animals. A passionate traveler, Chasity enjoys weaving glimpses of her real-life adventures into her stories. As an avid Anglophile, she adores all things British, with a particular love for the Regency era.

Born and raised in Tennessee, Chasity spent much of her childhood with her doting grandparents, where soap operas and back-to-back episodes of Scooby-Doo were part of her daily routine. Her path to becoming a romance novelist was perhaps inevitable—her Barbie dolls didn't just cruise in pink convertibles; they traveled through time, hosted extravagant dinner parties, and one even had an evil twin locked in the attic.

www.chasitybowlin.com